POINT CRIME

LAWLESS &
TILLEY

The Secrets of the Dead

MALCOLM ROSE

■SCHOLASTIC

For George, Kevin, Sue and Phil

Scholastic Children's Books
Commonwealth House, 1–19 New Oxford Street,
London WC1A 1NU, UK
a division of Scholastic Ltd
London ~ New York ~ Toronto ~ Sydney ~ Auckland

First published in the UK by Scholastic Ltd, 1997

Copyright © Malcolm Rose, 1997

ISBN 0 590 13371 3

Typeset by TW Typesetting, Midsomer Norton, Somerset
Printed by Cox & Wyman Ltd, Reading, Berks.

10 9 8 7 6 5 4 3 2 1

E dwyn Wragg stood on the high ridge of Hollins Cross and viewed the Vale of Edale that spread out luxuriously in front of him. "Beautiful," he murmured contentedly to himself. He was not yet aware that he was about to kindle one of the most disturbing murder inquiries ever undertaken by the South Yorkshire Police.

Below him, a country lane meandered beside the River Noe and past the snug village of Edale. In contrast, the straight line of the railway bisected the green valley precisely. To the east, it curved out of Edwyn's view towards Hope. To the west, where it came to the head of the valley, it disappeared into a hole in the hillside and burrowed under the High Peaks as if it had refused to deviate from its course. Just to the north of the entrance to Cowburn Tunnel,

1

crammed into a glen, there was the lonely and un-fashionable hamlet of Upper Needless – a small huddle of grey houses nestling together at the foot of Kinder Scout.

Filling his lungs with fresh summer air, Edwyn uttered, "This is what the world should be like. Idyllic. Unspoilt. What do you say, Murky?"

Murky was saying nothing. His long tongue hung from his mouth and dripped saliva happily.

Murky wasn't the collie's real name. Originally, Edwyn called him Mercury after the winged messenger of the gods. It seemed a good name because he was fast and he took great delight in bringing things to Edwyn, like discarded crisp packets and oily rags, as if they were gifts from heaven. Mercury sounded pompous, though, so it was abbreviated to Murky. For a dog that presented his master with so much disgusting rubbish, Murky seemed fitting as well.

"Let's get back to the camp site," Edwyn said.

The slope down from the ridge was steep but not precipitous. Three divergent tracks dropped down from the view point to different parts of the vale. Edwyn set out to the west along the footpath that traversed the hillside, lessening the downward gradient. It led directly to the camp site located alongside the railway cutting just before it pierced the peaks. As soon as Edwyn had selected the route, Murky brushed past his legs impatiently, eager to pretend that he was the pathfinder.

It was June. The bracken had not unfurled itself

and the heather remained camouflaged, not yet splashing the valley with colour. A small stream trickled down the slope, washing the pale outcrops of millstone grit and limestone. Scattered about the hillside, sheep grazed. The lambs were almost full grown and had a clean coat of white wool. The rest of the flock were newly shorn, with a small round patch of red dye on their flanks. The sheep watched Murky suspiciously but the dog showed no interest. Strangely for a collie, he had transferred his herding instinct to inanimate objects. It was less arduous to fetch aluminium cans than to torment sheep.

For a short distance, near the bottom of the slope, the footpath joined a dirt track and sliced through a long thin wood. Immediately, Murky ran off to investigate the intriguing smells. "Murky! Here, boy!" Edwyn called impotently. He'd long since learnt that, no matter how much he chided the dog, Murky would return only when he had completed his exploration. Edwyn shrugged and mumbled to himself, "Oh well. No rush."

Eventually, Murky ambled guiltily towards Edwyn to receive the usual ticking off.

On the other side of the copse, the barely distinguishable trail continued. Before it reached the floor of the glen and joined the road to Edale, it ran through another cluster of trees. "Stay close this time, Murky," Edwyn ordered.

The dog's remorse for his last indiscretion did not endure for long. Eagerly, he loped into the wood.

3

New place. New scents. Irresistible. The collie dashed from tree to tree, with his nose on the ground. Blindly, he followed the lingering traces of squirrels and foxes.

Resigned to his lack of control, Edwyn sighed and waited for Murky to have his fill. At first the dog remained in view but, as he became more engrossed with the invisible trails, he wandered out of Edwyn's sight. "Don't go far," Edwyn called into the grove. But it was too late. To Murky, his master's entreaty was less appealing than the smells of the spinney.

Edwyn waited patiently for five minutes and then boomed, "Murky! That's enough. Come here!"

Even at a distance from the track, Murky recognized Edwyn's tone as the final warning. He knew from painful experience that it was not worth disobeying that angry voice. Besides, he had sniffed out a prize and was ready to show it off. Retracing his steps and wagging his tail vigorously, he returned to Edwyn with something in his mouth.

"What have you got there?" Edwyn put out his hand. Eagerly and proudly, the collie placed his treasure on his master's outstretched palm.

At once, Edwyn dropped it, crying, "Ugh!" He turned away, groaning and wiping his hand as if he could erase the memory of the dog's find.

Murky was drooling over a severed human foot. It was partly decomposed, showing bite marks and exposed bones.

The idyllic valley had been spoilt after all.

Detective Superintendent John Macfarlane wiped the perspiration from his brow and neck with a crumpled handkerchief. When one of his sergeants approached, announcing that the Chief was on the car radio, he muttered wearily, "Doesn't he know we're off the beaten track here?"

Actually, the car was parked on the road not so far away but for a big lumbering man like John Macfarlane, it seemed like a laborious obstacle course. Instead, he extracted a mobile phone from a pocket and dialled. "Keith," he proclaimed. "You wanted me."

"How's it going? What's happening out there in my favourite bit of countryside? There's all sorts of rumours flying around here – and the press have got wind of them. What have we got?"

"Nothing pleasant about this particular bit of

5

countryside," John muttered. "Two bodies so far. Both male. Quite young, it seems. One's fairly fresh, I'd say, judging by the maggots. Foxes dragged him out of a shallow grave – and pulled him about a bit. The other's been here a while. Virtually skeletal. Both shot through the head. We're looking in case there's any more. But ... er ... more important than what we have got is what we haven't."

"What's that? You're not going to ask me for more officers, are you?"

"Of course I am. We've got a major job on here. We need to comb the ground for the weapon, empty casings and bullets. We need troops and lots of them. We need dogs. And we need entomologists – because we've got some seriously fat flies down here. Need I go on?"

"The dogs are no problem. I'll see what I can do about the rest," the Chief Superintendent replied in a tone that suggested it wouldn't be much. "I'll get on to forensics and have their bugs specialist sent to you. And ... oh ... I can allocate you an assistant."

"One?" Big John wailed.

"Look, Derbyshire Constabulary asked us to take on this case – even though it's in their area, not ours – because they haven't got the personnel or the resources to throw at it. We have – just. But I'm not that much better off in South Yorkshire, as you know. No slack in the system. Especially with this extra burden. So, one's all I've got, but he's ideal for the job."

"Oh yes?" John said sarcastically. "I know I'm going to regret asking, but why's that?"

"He's got a degree in biology. Or is it chemistry? Anyway, he probably knows all about maggots and corpses."

"What you're saying is you've got a new temporary inspector, one of those dreadful graduate entries, barely out of nappies and in serious need of on-the-job training. He's done his two years on the beat, passed the Special Course, and now you want me to break him in." John sighed. "This isn't the case for a raw recruit, Keith. I need someone who'll help the case, not hinder it. I want seasoned coppers. You know I've got no patience with these fast-track whizz-kids. Give him some domestic violence first. If he doesn't turn tail and run back to university, I'll take him then."

"No, John. He's promising – really. You know he must have something to get an attachment with us. Besides, he's all I've got for you. And he's as good as on his way."

Big John groaned. He knew that Keith was immovable. Reluctantly, he asked, "What's his name?"

"You're going to like this," Keith answered, chortling uncharacteristically. "He's called Lawless."

"You're joking," John exclaimed.

"No. Brett Lawless."

"B Lawless," John said scornfully. "That's all I need. A novice cop called Lawless. What are you trying to do to me, Keith?"

The Chief Superintendent responded with flattery. "If he's with you, I know he's in good hands."

"Just make sure he's got sturdy knee pads and a strong, fine comb," John quipped.

Keith laughed. "You'll find a proper outlet for his talents, I'm sure."

"You know I never jump to conclusions," Big John murmured. "First, I'll find out for myself if he's got any talent."

Brett drove out of Sheffield, through Hathersage and towards Hope, with mixed feelings. He seemed to have spent all of his twenty-six years in training for something. First, there were the long years at school that were supposed to be preparation for work and life. Because Brett was bright, it was expected that he would go to university. To refuse would have smacked of lack of ambition or confidence. He enjoyed science and he wanted to learn more about human beings, so for three years, he took a course in biochemistry. Because he graduated with a good degree, it was expected that he would go into research. This time, though, he rebelled. Startling all of his tutors, family and friends, he joined the police force instead. While the university course had taught him more and more about the bags of chemicals called humans, he found he knew less and less about real life. Also, as he approached the forefront of bio-chemical science, he became uneasy. He saw that science was already powerful enough in areas like genetic engineering – perhaps too powerful. It did not need his contribution.

In his five years in the police force, he'd been required to embark on more courses and to sit more exams. Sure, he'd also served his two years as a uniformed constable but, being on probation, he was given little responsibility. It still felt like preparation for the real thing. Because he passed his law exams with exceptionally high marks and possessed a flair for police work, his promotion was accelerated. He felt like a cheat, sneaking in the back door. Academically gifted but inexperienced, he had just been appointed to the rank of inspector, subject to a year's probation. He'd been assigned to the regional crime squad and was about to come under the supervision of a high-ranking CID officer, John Macfarlane. Brett hoped that, from here, the job would feel less like training and more like doing. But he was also aware that there was considerable resentment, even hostility, towards officers who used the Graduate Entry and Accelerated Promotion Schemes. While Brett understood such prejudices, he hoped that John Macfarlane did not share them. He did not relish a rough ride in his first substantial investigation.

The main road into Hope was blocked by an ancient car that had pulled out of the Edale turning and promptly broken down. The driver, an old man, tried to start the engine again but failed. A young motorist first sounded his horn twice, then flashed his headlights impatiently. Finally, he got out of his car and began to shout at the dithering old man. When the lad started to pound on the car roof with his fists, Brett decided that he had to act, before a charge of threatening behaviour became inevitable. As he approached, the confrontation was getting out of control. The youngster was yelling, "You're one of those weirdos from Upper Needless! Well, we don't need you in your crappy car. Go get your shopping somewhere else! We don't want you here."

Brett did not wish to be heavy-handed. He thought diplomacy would be preferable to police intervention. Besides, he was taller and broader than the irate youth. He hoped that his physical presence might intimidate the young driver. Interrupting the flow of abuse, Brett put in, "Look, instead of yelling insults, let's help everyone by pushing the car out of the way. If both of us do it, we'll have it on the forecourt of that garage up the road in a couple of minutes."

The youth glowered at Brett. "I'm not pushing this old crate anywhere. Round here, we don't want people like him." He nodded towards the quaking driver of the car.

Inside, the old man was so frightened that he locked the car door. This attempt at self-preservation seemed to enrage the young man even more. He crooked his arm and prepared to jab his elbow viciously through the glass of the window.

Brett had to intercede before the fragments of glass flew into the driver's pitiful face. "No!" he cried.

Just before the young man's elbow crashed into the window, Brett reached out and grabbed his wrist firmly, immediately checking the blow.

"Ow!" the lad squealed, as his arm jarred under Brett's powerful restraint. He yanked his wrist angrily out of Brett's grip.

Brett smiled at him and said, "Didn't want you to hurt yourself."

Realizing that he'd met his match, the young driver snarled, "You sort it out, then." Tempestuously, he retreated to his own car.

Brett ran his fingers through his thick black hair as he watched the teenager walk away. Recognizing that reconciliation was out of the question, Brett muttered regretfully, "Pity." Still, he'd averted an ugly affray. No harm had been done so he decided to let the lad go.

Bending down to look inside the vintage vehicle and about to address its vintage occupant, Brett hesitated. Beside the withered and bearded man there was a slender young woman, perhaps nineteen or twenty years of age. She was not wearing jewellery, make-up or fetching clothes, and her long black hair was rather untidy, but Brett's eyes were drawn irresistibly towards her. She was at the same time plain and extraordinarily beautiful. Before she turned her head away from him, there was a flicker of acknowledgement, of gratitude, on her face. Trying to concentrate on the mounting traffic problem, Brett knocked on the window and instructed the old man to release the handbrake. Taking a deep breath, he applied himself to the rear of the car. It moved forward only slowly at first but soon gathered momentum as Brett pushed hard. The time spent in rugby scrums first at school, then at university and now in the South Yorkshire police team was paying dividends. Between breaths, he called to the driver, "Steer it into the garage!" Once on the forecourt, Brett said, "They'll fix it for you here." Then he sprinted back to his own car, which was obstructing the road. The impetuous lad in the Mondeo had long since driven away at speed.

Brett got back into his car and turned right into the narrow lane to Edale. Away from the incident, he thought it strange that the old man with the stunning passenger had not uttered a single word. He hadn't replied to the insults hurled at him and he had not even communicated with Brett or thanked him. Brett shrugged. He did not linger on the encounter because it wasn't an auspicious start to his assignment.

On showing his warrant card, Brett was allowed through the police cordon just beyond Edale. He parked the car and a constable pointed out the way to the scene of the crime. It was four hundred metres from the road and well out of sight of the footpath. Before he introduced himself, Brett hesitated. A tranquil part of the countryside had been turned into a circus. A long blue and white police ribbon, stretching from tree to tree, encircled the terrain and fluttered like a perverse Christmas decoration.

Beyond the ribbon, many officers were on their hands and knees, scouring and sieving the floor of the wood for clues. In an orderly line, they were rummaging among the mass of dry twigs, last year's crispy brown leaves, soil, scavenging spiders and beetles. One officer was skimming the ground with a metal detector. A couple of sniffer dogs had just arrived and were going about their grisly business of tracking down more human remains.

"Well," Brett murmured to himself. "Here we go. The real thing."

Taking a deep breath, Brett ducked under the ribbon that divided normal life from the due process of law, the picturesque from the repulsive, the living from the dead. He strode up to one police officer and enquired, "Detective Superintendent John Macfarlane?"

"Yes," she said. "Over there." She pointed to a large, imposing man with a handkerchief glued to his left hand. He looked like the enormous queen at the quiet centre of a teeming termite nest. "The man with the fuller figure," she remarked wryly.

"Thanks," Brett replied.

As he approached the Superintendent, he announced his presence by saying, "Sir?"

"Yes," John Macfarlane replied in a curt, business-like tone. "Who are you?"

"Brett Lawless," he declared. "I think you're expecting me to report to you."

"Ah, yes," he responded. "The professor." His tone suggested mockery.

Instantly, any notion of an easy ride disappeared. Plainly, John Macfarlane did not approve of young graduate officers.

"Welcome aboard," he said, without conviction. "They've pushed you in at the deep end, no mistake. When we start the inquiries proper, I'll have plenty for you to do, but for now, just keep close and keep your eyes open. Familiarize yourself with the case. Can you manage that?" he added derisively.

"I'll do my best," Brett retorted, not hiding the bitterness in his voice.

John ignored his apprentice's discontent. "I hope your stomach's as strong as your brain. We've got an unsavoury one here." He pointed further into the wood and grunted, "Come on. I'll introduce you to Victim Number One, as he's known."

The body was a grotesque dry shell of a human being, barely more than a skeleton with scraps of brown leathery skin adhering to it. The head had been disturbed by rats or foxes and the cracked skull lay several centimetres away from the trunk. The victim had been hidden crudely by branches and dead leaves. Now the skeleton lay in the open and the entomologist was kneeling beside it, plucking out live insects and pupal cases with tweezers. She bagged each one carefully for examination in the laboratory later.

"Well?" Big John prompted.

Dressed from head to foot in a pure white overall, Sue Kilbracken was holding a small yellow insect on her tweezers and peering at it closely. "*Tineola biselliella*, the common clothes moth," she concluded. "Once he's had his fill here, he'll be into your wardrobe." She smiled enthusiastically and popped him into a small plastic box. When she looked up, she noticed Brett for the first time. She caught her breath momentarily before continuing: "The human body's a wonderful resource. A reservoir of food for insects, and a wonderful nursery for their young. They can chomp through it – recycling at its best – faster than a couple of lions."

"Yes," John replied. "But how long's this particular natural resource been here?"

"Besides the clothes moths, there's mites, fur beetles and carpet beetles. I need a closer examination of the pupal cases before I can identify them all. They might tell me more. But there's no mealworm beetles, so it's only about a year old. Definitely less than sixteen months," she estimated confidently.

"What about Victim Number Two?"

"An interesting one, that," Sue proclaimed. "Pathology wants an old date – some of the tissues are liquefying nicely already. Advanced decay. But I'm not happy about it." Standing up, she said, "Let's take a look and I'll show you what I mean." She was a short, dumpy woman in her early forties. Instantly likeable, she was bursting with personality and her round, jovial face belied the horrors that she examined. She breezed towards the second insect farm.

The body seemed to be trying to escape from a shallow grave, like the undead in a horror film. Parts of it were still buried, but most of it had emerged into the air. The foot from the left leg was missing and the right arm had been dragged some distance away, and showed clear signs of having been chewed. In his short time with the police, Brett had seen death before, but nothing like this. The victim's face was a living, moving mask of maggots. Brett swallowed uncomfortably.

"Foraging foxes unearthed him and have already had their wilful way with him," Sue began. "As you can see, there's an infestation of bluebottle and housefly maggots. Hungry little chappies. In hot weather like this, they colonize a body and eat for twenty-four hours a day, accounting for half its volume in about a week. Wonderful cleaners of carrion. Anyway, it looks quite old – and it's covered in some white substance that's got me beat at the moment – but after ten days a decomposing body doesn't give off the chemicals that attract bluebottles. Each female bluebottle will lay a couple of hundred eggs, mostly around the moist areas like the eyes, mouth and nose. They hatch after fifteen hours and the maggots start their banquet. Hence the pile of them on his face. They increase in size about ten times and then transform into pupae. Quite a few of the chappies in here have moulted once or twice but they're not yet ready for the pupal stage. Even if the degree of decay is surprising, the insect evidence is unequivocal. Your man's been here a week or two at most. Once I age the maggots, I'll pin this one down even further," she reported.

"What about the white stuff?" Brett queried.

"I'm taking some back to the labs to identify it."

Trying to conceal his queasiness and revulsion, Brett bent down and examined some of the remaining flesh on the left arm. "Any chance it's some sort of fungus?" he asked.

Sue smiled at him, impressed by his interest and struck by his suggestion. "Possibly," she answered. "I've never seen it before."

"Keep us in touch," Big John requested.

From another part of the wood, there was a cry for the guvnor. Taking the entomologist and Brett with him, he ambled in the direction of the shout. He passed two ashen-faced sergeants before one of the dog handlers announced, "Another two bodies for you. Again, they're just under branches."

"Let's take a look," John said, dabbing at his brow. "You know what I want," he said to his team of officers. "Photographs of everything as you take the branches away."

"You're not going to like it, sir," a sergeant guessed. "One's just a kid. A baby."

John sighed. "I'm not fond of any killing."

Big John and Brett watched as the bodies of a

woman and a child were gradually exposed. They were concealed between two beech trees. The trunk of one was twisted like an old church spire and two of its branches were strangely entwined like the strands of DNA. The other beech leaned menacingly towards Brett. Its branches grew outwards and upwards, forming large U-shaped loops. They were warped evilly, like the mind of the murderer.

Brett protected himself from the cruelty by reminding himself that the victims died quickly. If there had to be a death, a shot through the head was about as clean as it could be. As for what followed – decay – Brett tried to regard it merely as nature at work. The biochemist in him knew that the end of human life was the cessation of one series of chemical reactions and the beginning of a different set. Death was not an end, but a change. Metabolism gave way to putrefaction. The spent human body became the host for the next generation of insect life. It was easy in a lecture room to think of death as a transform-ation, nurturing new life, but remaining dispassion-ate when confronted with it was a different matter. The process should have been a glorious rebirth but, in the field, it was a gory invasion of the human form.

As soon as the remains of the child's pitifully small body were uncovered, as soon as Brett saw the tiny exposed bones of the hands, he turned to one side and vomited profusely.

John Macfarlane eyed him with a degree of both contempt and compassion.

"Sorry," Brett mumbled, wiping his mouth. "It's ... er ... I don't know. It's the baby, I guess. I can take anything but that."

"Mmm." Detective Superintendent Macfarlane admitted, "Most of me wants to lecture you about being detached and professional, but there's a bit of me that regrets not throwing up as well. Any normal person would. But you'd better get used to the idea that police officers aren't normal. You'd better get anaesthetized to cruelty."

Brett was not sure why he had reacted so badly to the sight of a young death. It was as if the shock had evoked some distant and dreadful memory, without actually having the power to bring back a terrifying image. He was left feeling unsettled, empty and inadequate.

After his initial examination, the forensic pathologist reported that the woman was quite young. "Mid to late teens, judging by the teeth," he estimated. "Just like the male victims. Again, I need to get a clean look at something like the femur to check ossification – but I don't think it's complete in any of them."

Brett knew that, in infancy, humans developed an accessory bone called an epiphysis at certain joints. It was attached to the main shaft by cartilage. By the end of the teens, the cartilage would be fused to the main structure by converting to bone. The precise extent of this ossification could be used to measure age to within a year or so. If it was incomplete, the victim would be aged nineteen or under.

"She's been shot through the side of the head at point-blank range like the others. Bullet in one side and straight out the other. Possibly point three eight calibre. Also like the other victims," the pathologist continued impassively. "The baby's no more than a few weeks. Probably male. Shot through the head again. This time, the skull's shattered. Suggests the gun was placed right against the head. When fired, the gas pressure exploded the skull."

They all looked up as two military aircraft hurtled through the valley, directly overhead. One following the other, they were flying so low that they weaved between the Peaks as if they were taking part in some dangerous high-speed aerial chase for a spectacular film stunt. The engines roared so loudly that they obliterated all conversation. The racket dissolved the Detective Superintendent's curse.

As soon as the jets climbed over the ridge of Hollins Cross and then descended into another valley to plague someone else, John snorted, "Military training exercises!" Turning his attention back to the carcasses, he surmised grimly, "What we have here is a series of executions. Have they all been shot from the same side?" he asked the doctor.

"No. Some entrance wounds are on the right, some on the left. I'll have to reconstruct the child's skull before I can trace the bullet's path. In the others, the exit wounds are similar — enlarged by bone fragments carried with the bullet. Could be the same gun. Could be different. No sign of a struggle by any of the victims, either."

They were anonymous and seemed determined to remain so. There was no jewellery, no identifying features, no bags, no documents.

"Dental records won't help you with identification," the pathologist noted. "Not perfect teeth but not a filling between the three older subjects. And all the bodies are too far gone for fingerprints."

Big John motioned to Sue. "Go in now and tell me what you find."

While he waited for Sue to finish her inspection, John said to his new assistant, "You might as well know from the outset, I don't believe there's a quick way to becoming a decent copper—"

Interrupting, Brett remarked with a grin, "I'd gathered that."

John did not return his smile. He continued, "A long, hard slog's the only way. You don't get there just by passing exams. You learn the trade by doing it, sometimes making mistakes, building up your experience."

Brett nodded. "That's why I'm here."

"Yes, but you're an inspector now, at least a probationary one. It's a bit late. Constables and sergeants make mistakes. No one expects an officer holding the rank of inspector to foul it up – especially not on a high-profile murder case."

Determined not to be browbeaten by his commanding officer, Brett remarked, "I can see I've got a lot of work to do to prove my credentials."

"I'll tell you what you need to make a good police officer," the Superintendent preached. "One: you've got to understand people. That's the most important thing. Two: you've got to be a careful observer. Three: you've got to interpret facts creatively. Finally: you've got to be a good team player. Degrees and exams don't give you that."

Defending himself assertively, Brett replied, "You'd be surprised. Biochemistry gave me quite a few of those things. Science is all about observing, deducing logically and being creative."

"Yeah, but it doesn't help you get inside the mind of whoever did this." He spread out his arms to indicate the carnage in the wood. Then he tapped the side of his head and added, "It doesn't help you to think like a crook."

Sue Kilbracken called them over to the bodies. As they approached, Brett kept his eyes averted from the baby's corpse.

"Fairly straightforward," she disclosed. "About three months old, these. The fats are rancid. You can smell they're a bit cheesy. There's larder beetles, a few flesh-flies, tabby moths and devil's coach-horses. That's a type of beetle. Necrobia beetles and lesser dung flies haven't got a foothold yet. You can be pretty certain about their time of death: both the same, three months ago. They've both attracted my favourite maggots, *Piophila casei*. Acrobatic little chappies. They're only small, five or six millimetres, called cheesekippers. Watch." She brought a branch down towards the exposed decaying flesh. "When they're disturbed they curl up and grab their own rears with their mouths. When they let go, like coiled springs, they skip into the air six inches or so. See?"

A few tiny yellow maggots leapt from the body when Sue threatened them with the stick.

"Not particularly useful when judging the time of death, but amusing little blighters. Super escape mechanism."

"Thanks, Sue," John replied. "Very helpful. I'll get your full report later, no doubt."

"Yes. Once I've examined everything properly back in the labs, I might be able to give you more."

Big John looked up through the branches at the clear blue sky and bright sun. "God, it's hot," he gasped. "Right. Let's think what we've got here – and renumber the victims. One male shot through the head at close range one year ago: Victim number One. Now Victims Number Two and Three are the young woman and the baby. Killed at the same time three months ago. Also shot in the head. The biologists will soon tell us if it's mother and son. DNA fingerprinting."

Brett interjected, "Only if there's still some good-quality DNA. It might all be degraded by now."

"They can work wonders with hair roots," John commented. Then, continuing the obscene catalogue, he said, "Finally, there's the one we called Victim Number Two. Actually, he's Victim Number Four. A juvenile, shot perhaps ten days ago. It all

24

adds up to some sort of ritual, serial killing," he inferred. "So where are we going to start?"

"Identities of the victims," Brett suggested.

"OK. Where are they from, and what links them – apart from murder?"

"That'll need research," Brett responded.

"Well, they're not all from around here, I'd say. Four people missing from a small community would've already caused some consternation. I've asked the local police. There aren't any missing persons from round here. So, we'll need all the victims' details in the computer and a search against the nationwide database of missing persons."

"You're thinking they could be tourists?"

"Maybe," John answered. "But I've no evidence yet that they were killed here. No empty shells and no bullets. We might have stumbled across the grave-yard, not the killing fields themselves. Maybe they're all from London – or Sheffield. We need the link. With serial killers like this there's always something that links their prey." The detective plonked himself down on a horizontal log. "So much for the victims. What about the crime? Which of the murders are you going to prioritize?"

Brett thought about it for a moment. "Victim Number Three. The baby," he decided. "Babies are conspicuous things. Everyone notices when one goes missing."

"Mmm." John considered Brett's opinion for a few seconds. "No," he concluded. "We need to know something about them all but we'll concentrate on Victim Number Four. The disappearance of a baby might be conspicuous at the time but it was three months ago. People's memories are awful on the whole. We start with the freshest victim. If he was killed only ten days ago, his disappearance will still be in everyone's mind."

Brett shrugged. "OK. I'm just concerned about his body. It's covered in something white and looks older than a couple of weeks. I wonder if we're dealing with too many unknowns with him."

John raised his eyebrows. "No. I trust Sue – and the maggots. He hasn't been around for long. We lead with him – the freshest. I don't like old victims. Experience has shown me that they don't live long in the memory. Now," he added, "what about the killer – or killers? It's someone who's been here at least three times. A year ago, three months ago and just recently."

"Could be a local or maybe a tourist who keeps coming back."

"Yes. This place is near enough to the road to be a favourite haunt of a passing tourist and a psychopath – with a vehicle. The victims could be alive or dead when they come here. In the middle of the night, it wouldn't be too difficult to drag a dead body from a car on the road to here. At least for someone fitter than me," Big John remarked. "It's not that far. A local might choose an even more secluded spot to dispose of bodies. Still, it's probably remote enough for a local to use it. We need to check out both. I can leave the tourists for you to cover. We need names and addresses of everyone using hotels, bed and breakfasts, camp sites in the last, say, sixteen months. We'd interview anyone who was here last year, three months ago and a few days ago. The trouble is, the camp sites won't keep a record of everyone who pitches a tent in their field for a night or two. Anyway, our murderer would have to be pretty dim to get caught by collecting names from guest houses. We'll probably be wasting our time. Still," John explained, "ninety-nine per cent of the job is painstaking, boring routine that yields nothing at all. That's what it's all about. Nit-picking. Everyone looks to the CID for glamour, excitement and danger. That's the effect of the telly. Except on the box, the moments of excitement and inspiration are few and far between. One per cent of the job."

"What about the chap who said he discovered the bodies?" Brett enquired. "Always the first suspect, whoever finds the bodies."

"Yes. Some killers do report finding their victims. They think it deflects suspicion. Serial killers in particular have been known to inject themselves into the investigation of their murder victims. They appear to be helpful to the case but really they're making it a game between themselves and us. But I spoke to Edwyn Wragg. He was genuinely shocked. Distraught. I've got his address – just in case – but he's not our man. He's just an ordinary bloke with an inquisitive collie."

A dog handler emerged from behind an old oak and reported, "We're done. The dogs haven't found any more. Bits of clothing and flesh from one of the other victims, two birds' nests made of hair from the woman, but no new bodies. You've got all the victims you're going to get."

"Quite enough for one day," John rejoined. "Thanks. You can go."

Wheezing, he stood up. He put an assistant called Greg Lenton in charge of the proceedings in the wood and let the scene-of-the-crime team and the forensic scientists go about their business. "Come on," he said to Brett. "You can drive me."

"Where to?"

"Distraction, probably." The old detective smiled slyly.

John Macfarlane was a heavyweight. At twenty stone, he wasn't the most sprightly detective but he was immensely perceptive and his podgy hands were very safe. He had an enviable record for cracking awkward cases, albeit at his own deliberate pace.

In uniform, on the beat, Brett had learned to walk slowly, but it wasn't slow enough for John Macfarlane's laboured gait. As they neared the lane John said, "I want you to drive up the road a bit, turn round, and come back."

Brett looked puzzled. "Why?"

"You'll see."

As the Superintendent squeezed into the car, it rocked alarmingly. More athletic, Brett slipped into the driver's seat and turned on the ignition.

"Just up to where we've blocked the road," John requested.

While Brett executed a three-point turn in a passing place, Big John said, "Right. You've just shot your victim. He's in the boot. Or maybe I'm your victim — alive but unsuspecting — in the passenger seat. You're approaching your favourite home-made burial site. What are you going to do?"

"I'd park the car as close as I could to the wood but only if there was a discreet stopping place. Somewhere the car wouldn't be too noticeable. I'd sacrifice a bit of distance for discretion."

"So would I," John agreed. "Let's find it, then."

Police cars and vans littered the hedgerows. Brett and John ignored them, trying to locate a likely parking spot.

Just before the spinney, there was a dirt track. "Probably leads to a farm," John muttered. "Pull into it."

Brett manoeuvred the car on to the track and then stopped. "Yes, I might have tried here. The ground's hard on my side, I could park behind the hedge." He put the car into first gear to try out his idea.

"No, no," John barked. "Let's look on foot first."

The Detective Superintendent stood to one side gazing at the potential parking place but not encroaching on it. "Yes," he murmured. "I want forensics here once they're done in the wood. No hope of tyre marks but someone's emptied an ashtray of fag ends over there. See? And look at that fence post. Near the bottom. Yes? There's some silver paint on it. Perhaps a car's scraped against it. They'll identify the paint and make of car, if that's what it is." Gingerly, he stepped towards the cigarette butts. Without touching anything, he peered at them. "Benson and Hedges, and Silk Cut," he muttered. "Faint lipstick on the Silk Cut." He retreated towards the car. Before they set off again, he radioed to the forensic team in the wood and explained carefully what he wanted them to tackle next.

When Brett began to reverse back out into the lane, John queried, "What are you doing now?"

"Just because we've got one likely spot, it doesn't mean there's not a better one just down the road," answered Brett emphatically.

"True enough," John consented. "We'll take a look and *then* come back to have a word with the farmer – or whoever's at the end of this track. Hope it is a farmer," he said, "because they're the easiest people in the world to interview. You just let them go on about the weather, government subsidies, and hours of work. Sympathize and they're putty in your hands."

Within five hundred metres of the wood, there were no other likely sites to park a car unobtrusively. Instead, Brett drove back to the track and continued along it until they came to an old, unkempt farmhouse where frantic barking announced their arrival. Inside, the unpleasant smell of dogs pervaded the cold, drab and uncarpeted living room. John settled himself into a shabby armchair that was coated with fine black Labrador hairs, and explained to the farmer why hordes of police officers had arrived in the area. He apologized for any inconvenience. "It's a bit rich for us to add to everything else you have to put up with," he ventured.

The owner of the house, a middle-aged man called George Bottomley, recognized his cue instantly. Being a sheep farmer, he did not grumble about the vagaries of the English weather but launched into a tirade against the price of lamb, the hazards of sheep dip, tourists' dogs, and antisocial working hours.

Brett would have interrupted to ask his questions but John seemed to possess infinite patience. He was content to listen earnestly, nod and tut at the appropriate places. Eventually, he said, "And then we come and trample all over the place. Still," he added, "we won't be long now, but we've got to get to the bottom of it. I'm sure you'll appreciate that."

Tamed by John, George agreed.

"I was hoping you might have seen something out of the ordinary in the last couple of weeks, especially at odd times. Late at night, early in the morning. Any unusual activity," John prompted.

The farmer pondered on it. "No," he answered. "Can't say I have. That's despite keeping my eyes open for the last few months."

"Why do you say that?"

"Some of my sheep have been going missing. It's not dogs this time because there's been no carcasses. Someone's been stealing them. Just you wait till I get my hands on whoever's doing it."

"I'm sorry to hear that," Brett said. Trying to

muscle in on the interview and keep the farmer to the point, he asked, "Your dogs haven't started barking in the middle of the night or anything?"

"No. Quiet as mice."

"How about a car at the end of your drive?" John enquired.

"Plenty miss the turning up to the camp sites," the farmer replied. "They pull into my drive to turn round."

"Annoying," John commiserated. "But have you seen one stop there for any length of time?"

"Not so I noticed," said George.

"Do you have any silver vehicles yourself?" asked the Detective Superintendent.

"Silver? No. Bit too posh for the farm."

"Are you a married man? With kids?"

"Yes," George replied. "Two boys. Fourteen and fifteen. They help around the farm. They've gone into Hope just now, though."

"Do any of them smoke, your wife or the boys?"

"We can't afford cigarettes in this household," George moaned. "And we can't afford to risk our health. Who knows what would happen to the farm if any of us got sick."

"Have you heard any guns being fired?" John queried.

"Of course. There's often shooting in the Vale. I've fired a few myself. All above board, like," George added quickly. "Foxes, rabbits, the occasional dog that worries the sheep. That sort of thing."

"So you wouldn't take much notice of shots?"

"Not a lot."

"What about at night?"

"Can't recall any firing at night," George replied. "What would be the point of shooting in the dark?" Then he continued, "Oh, yes. Of course. Your victims might have been shot at night. No. I haven't heard anything, but I sleep soundly after a long day's work."

"Your wife or sons haven't mentioned hearing anything in the night – in the last couple of weeks or so?" Brett put in.

"No. Nothing at all," he responded.

John struggled to his feet, murmuring, "Well, I think we've bothered you enough for one day. We've taken up too much of your busy time already."

George Bottomley glanced at his watch. "Yes, I must be getting on. But I'm pleased to help, if I can."

"Thanks," John puffed. "But we'll leave you in peace for now."

In the gloomy hallway, George said, "You could help me as well. As you go around, keep your eyes peeled for my sheep, will you? You can't miss them. Red dye on the right flank." With restrained anger in his voice, he muttered, "I want to know who's rustling them. Costing me a fortune."

Back inside the car, Brett said to his superior, "You don't think a farmer would resort to killing sheep rustlers on his land, do you?"

John grinned. "People kill for all sorts of reasons.

I once arrested a husband who'd murdered his wife for burning a hole in one of his shirts when she was ironing it. Such trivial things are usually the final provocation in a long line of quibbles – the last straw. Perhaps George Bottomley is at the end of his tether as well, but he wouldn't tell us about it if he'd killed four people for rustling. Besides, a moment's thought would tell you that babies don't steal sheep."

"True." Brett tried to ignore the implied insult.

It was early evening when they drove back on to the road. "There's no question about our next move," John commented.

"Oh?" Brett responded. "What's that?"

"A pie and a pint in the pub at Edale. Just by the start of the Pennine Way."

Brett smiled and nodded. "OK."

"While I have it," John proclaimed, "you can begin your inquiries at the camp site there."

For an instant, Brett looked askance at his boss. "The way you've been doubting me," he wisecracked wickedly, "I'm surprised you don't send *me* to the pub while you get on and do a proper job."

John laughed aloud. "There's hope for you yet! At least you can take a joke. In this job you need to get used to jokes at your expense – and give as much needle as you get. Anyway, let's get those pies down our throats. The hotels, guest houses and camp sites can wait till tomorrow."

The radio burst into life at 6.15am, filling Brett's bedroom with the early-morning news. It included a brief report on the gruesome find of several human corpses in a wood near Edale. "The police have not yet confirmed that they have set up a high-level murder hunt. They plan to release details at a news conference later today." Brett groaned. He felt as if the item had thrust him into work even before he was fully awake.

He got up and dressed in shorts, vest and running shoes. Every day before breakfast he relaxed by jogging round the perimeter of the park. It was a distance of about two miles. A gentle early run always made him feel alive, fit and fresh. He used the exercise to try to cleanse himself of the ugly images and tragic acts that lodged in his police officer's mind. He could not afford to be drained by sad lives and sad deaths, sheer cruelty, the remains of fragile human beings. He could not afford to be tainted by the crime that he witnessed. To relieve the tension, to stay sane among so much insanity, he had to have a mechanism to distance himself from the worst violence that one human being could inflict on another. While he ran, though, he would often think about his punishing job. He knew that, as always, chance circumstances and not plans would dictate his working hours. His early-morning routine was the only predictable part of his day. He enjoyed the constant twists and turns of police work. He enjoyed the challenge. But occasionally he also doubted that he was capable of meeting it. Yesterday was one of those times. Doubt had entered his head as soon as he'd seen the baby's body. He found it difficult enough to confront murder without a helpless child being among the casualties.

As he pounded impressively round the park, he forced himself to think about different challenges. He had an ambition to take part in a marathon one day, but the demands of his job always blocked the way. He also thought about his parents. A challenge of a different kind. They lived miles away in Kent. He hadn't seen them for more than a year and he had last spoken to them by phone at Christmas. That, and a phone call on each of their birthdays, seemed to satisfy them. They never invited him down to Kent, and whenever he asked them to visit him in

Sheffield, they cited their dislike of travelling as an excuse. But there was more than that. Even when he was young, he had never got on well with his parents. They had always been cool towards him. It was as if he had once broken an irreplaceable ornament and they had been unable to forgive him. Brett could not remember all of the naughty things he might have done as a child and his parents seemed unable to talk about the inexcusable sin that he felt he must have committed. He had long since suppressed any such memory. Now, as he strode along the footpath, he wondered how long his parents could bear a grudge against their only child. If it could last for twenty years, perhaps it would persist for a lifetime. Whenever he thought of his parents, he always ended up feeling both irritated and guilty.

Breathing deeply, but not tired, he returned to his house. He shaved, took a brisk shower and then tucked into a swift breakfast. In the lounge, he fed the fish in his aquarium. For a while, he watched the large and stately discus fish. Uncannily still, it hung in the water while the smaller and brighter guppies and tetras darted all around it, foraging for invisible food. Immediately, Brett was reminded of the turmoil in the wood. At its epicentre, Big John Macfarlane had been motionless while the rest of the team had flitted here and there, scavenging for clues.

Brett tore himself away from the calm of his aquarium. It was time to join the real world, to scavenge for more clues.

John Macfarlane had assembled the core of the team in one room in the Sheffield Headquarters. It was 8am and strangely subdued. The sixteen officers murmured to their neighbours rather than trading banter right across the room. As a newcomer and a stranger, Brett was excluded from the fractured conversations.

"OK," John began his briefing. "We're all here. Thanks for being prompt. We've got a heavy day in front of us. Possibly a heavy few weeks. We all know each other, I think, except for Brett here." John pointed him out. "I'm sure you'll all treat him as well as a probationary detective inspector deserves to be treated." There was humour, irony and a sting in John's voice. "Brett, you'll meet all the others as you go along, OK?" Without waiting for a reply, he said, "That'll give everyone enough time to work out their own hilarious witticism on Brett's surname – Lawless. But it's my guess Brett will have heard it all before over the last few years in the force. Now," he continued, "we do have serious business. A cash-strapped Derbyshire's asked us to take this case on. It's close to us and the Chief's agreed so it's ours. As you all know, we have four unidentified bodies. All shot at more-or-less point-blank range through the head. Two young men, probably teenagers, a young woman also believed to be in her teens and, I've no need to remind you, a new-born baby. Since there wasn't a gun by any of the bodies, we can rule out suicide. Besides, babies don't commit suicide. Given that there were no bullets or casings either, they may have been shot elsewhere. We're calling them Victim Number One to Victim Number Four, in order of death, till we get identities. Details – such as they are – are on the wall over there. By the way, thanks to Mark and Clare who sat up most of the night organizing our fine base camp."

On the wall, there was a whiteboard divided into four. There was one section for each victim. Gender, approximate time of death, a description of clothing and hair, height, probable weight, and rough age had been written in. The most important spaces – for names, addresses and common links – were depressingly blank. Next to the whiteboard, a large-scale map of the Vale of the Edale was pinned to the wall. A cluster of four red dots marked the slovenly burial ground. The room was equipped with six telephones, a fax machine, myriad filing cabinets, several computer terminals, and a mound of reference material such as maps, directories and tourist information on the Peak District.

"Priorities," the Detective Superintendent was saying. "Identities. All four victims are equally important. As the lab reports come in, details straight into the computer. They're unlikely to be local, so search nationwide. In particular, we want the link between them. There has to be a pattern to all this. Once we know that, we're most of the way towards a motive. Mark and Liz, you're in charge of computing. There's a lot of forensic evidence on this one. I want you, Brett, to liaise with forensic. New or refined info on victims goes directly to Mark and Liz and on to the wall for us all to see. Anything on suspects, like the silver car, comes to me. Now, the murders themselves. Any leads on the older ones are likely to be cold. For the moment, we concentrate on Victim Number Four. Killed less than two weeks ago. So we ask around. Take his description – clothes, height and so on – from the whiteboard. The nearest we'll get to door-to-door inquiries is asking around at the camp sites, local shops, pubs and so on. OK? We need to jog people's memories while there's still something to jog, so let's make this one snappy. I'll put you eight on to it. Organize it so you cover the ground today and tomorrow.

"Lastly, there's our culprit. Let's not forget him – or her, or them. Seems like we're after a serial killer. Since nearly all serial killers are white men, we'll call our man 'him', but also keep an open mind. Anyway, we want to arrest him before we have to investigate Victim Number Five. Now, for those of you who are new to this sort of investigation," he said, glancing at Brett, "serial killers normally come in four flavours. One: the power and control junkies. They need to torment, torture and control other people. Unlikely in this case because there was no indication of struggles or other wounds. Two: the thrill-seekers. Those who get their kicks from killing instead of drawing the line at driving fast or drinking alcohol like the rest of us. Both of these categories can involve sexual assaults as well. Judging by the clothing, or remnants of it, all our victims were fully dressed so we can probably rule out a sexual motive. Three: the listeners. These are the ones that swear God or demons have whispered in their ears, giving them a holy – or unholy – mission to kill. Could be. No evidence against that one. Four: the cleaners. They take it upon themselves to rid the world of 'undesirables'. So, they set out to murder tramps, for instance. Obviously, all their victims have something in common. Again, we've nothing to refute it. At least we know he's not after teenagers, because of the baby, or just one gender, because he's gone for both. My money's on a cleaner or a listener. Or both. If the victims were undesirables in our man's eyes, maybe God told him to destroy them. Whichever variety we've got, even if we've got ourselves a new species altogether, we can take it that he's a methodical, organized killer. He's mad or bad. We don't know which. Generally, psychologists say serial killers are insane, juries tend to say they're evil. One thing's for sure – he's someone with no sense of responsibility to anyone or anything, except his own, probably limited, circle."

Big John concluded, "Our man could be a local or a tourist. Let's check out the tourist angle first. It's easier. You know the current best estimates of times of death. Let's see if they match with the visits of any regular tourists. We'll need a good few of you on this as well, cruising the guest houses and the like. Brett, that's one for you. Get together a team and make sure you cover all tourist accommodation in the Vale."

"Sir?" Greg Lenton piped up. "Permission to join the team chasing identities?"

Big John paused, grimaced and then responded, "If you've got a problem working with a probationary inspector, just sort it out. That goes for you all. I'm not organizing the squad according to personalities. We've got more important things to worry about. You're working with Brett, Greg. OK?"

Greg snorted. "OK," he mumbled.

Disappointed, but not surprised, Brett sighed. He glanced towards the ceiling, closed his eyes, took a deep breath and tried to ignore Greg's attempt to undermine his status in the squad.

John looked at his watch. "Right. You're on your own till lunch. I've got to bring the Chief up to date and then face the firing squad."

Puzzled, Brett frowned. Next to him, the Detective Sergeant called Clare whispered, "Face the press, he means. Not his favourite occupation, press conferences."

Clare was about the same age as Brett but a couple of inches shorter, so she was probably five feet eleven. She was attractive, with light skin and short, startlingly red hair, and Brett was grateful to her for drawing him into the team rather than isolating him.

Brett gathered about him the five officers and first asked their names. He was blessed with the ability never to forget a name and this had always helped him relate to a team. "Well," he started. "You heard the boss. We need names and addresses of visitors to the area. I doubt if camp sites keep a note of names, but we'll try them anyway. We'll do better with guest houses, hotels, rented accommodation and the rest of it. I don't know how long they keep records, but we should particularly target three time windows. A year to sixteen months ago – let's say March to July last year. Then there's three months ago – we'll cover February to April. That's our best bet since there'll be fewer tourists about. Then there's the last couple of weeks. You know John wants us to focus on this one. I agree. It's a good lead but let's remember that, while there's not much doubt about the time of death of the first three victims, Victim Number Four's not so clear-cut. Let's bear that in mind and not become too dependent on the last victim."

"So you want us to ignore the guvnor?" one of the team asked pointedly, testing him.

"Lawless by name…" Greg put in coldly.

Brett knew that his colleagues were not teasing. They were not indulging in the jokes that John had said that he would have to get used to. There was real hostility behind their taunts. He smiled sarcastically and replied firmly, "No. That's not what I said. I just want us to note that pathology and the insect evidence don't agree. There's some dispute about the time of death of the latest victim. I'll confirm it with forensics as soon as I can. Besides, I'm not asking you to collate any information in the field. Don't ditch any names because they weren't there in the last fortnight. Just bring back complete lists that cover our time windows. We'll let the computer cross-check them because if our man's a tourist he might have stayed in different places each time. After that, we'll follow up anyone who hits two or three of our time zones – that's all I'm saying. That way, we'll get a good list of suspects even if Victim Number Four's an older corpse than the present estimate. In fact, if you get complete lists from February last year to today, we'll have it all covered, no matter what." Brett glanced round at the sullen faces. There was no further audible dissent. "Right. Let's trawl the tourist information first. Get ourselves organized with lists of accommodation. There's only six of us. Five, if I'm off chasing forensics. That's two pairs out in the field. One pair covers Castleton and everything to the east, the other pair does all places west of Castleton. The other's on the phone tracing the owners of rented accommodation and private holiday homes, working with me to interview them and to butter up the Tourist Board for more information."

Really, Brett wanted to select Clare Tilley as his partner. She seemed to be the most genial of the bunch. Yet he recognized that he had to convince his more antagonistic colleagues of his worth. "Greg," he said, "you partner me. I can tell you've got a lovely telephone manner." When he delivered the gibe, only Clare chuckled. "Finally," he added earnestly, "let's cheer up and start acting like a team – all pulling in the same direction."

On her way out, Clare slapped Brett on the arm and said quietly, "Welcome to the testosterone club!"

Just after Clare and the other three officers left for Edale, the first report came in by fax from the Forensic Department. When he read it, Brett murmured happily to himself, "Yes!" Directly, he made for Mark and Liz. "Our first bit of luck," he announced. "Both good and bad, but mainly good. The silver paint's definitely from a Mercedes-Benz."

"Classy cars," Mark commented drily. "Which model is it?"

"That's the bad news. The silver's used across the full range of Mercedes. We don't know the model. But there's more good news. That particular paint was introduced only recently. It's an environmentally friendly water-based paint. Forensically friendly as well. Get on to it, will you? We need a list of all owners of new silver Mercedes models."

More affable than Mark, Liz replied, "Expensive runabouts. There won't be that many on the road. Should be a doddle to narrow it down."

"What's more," Brett added gleefully, "owners of Mercs don't pitch tents. They stay in hotels. So, as long as the driver stayed overnight, we stand a chance of having his or her name on one of our hotel lists. When those lists start coming in, get the computer to cross-check them with the car owners.

I'd be interested, to say the least, if one name cropped up on both lists."

As soon as Brett walked away, Greg leant on Mark's shoulder playfully and said, "He's got a BSc, you know." Clearly, he was referring caustically to Brett. "What do you think it stands for? Back to Special Constable?"

Mark chuckled. "Back to School Classes is even better."

"How about Big Sir's Calamity?" Greg suggested.

Liz said to her colleagues, "Don't you think you're Being Somewhat Cruel?"

Greg and Mark laughed. "Very good. But no. Not cruel. Just ... unconvinced."

After the initial burst of activity, the incident room seemed becalmed like a boat adrift on a still sea. Mark and Liz tapped keyboards softly. Greg telephoned an endless succession of owners of rented accommodation and holiday cottages, noting their addresses so that he could visit them later to obtain lists of clients and dates of visits. Once the press conference had been broadcast on television, Greg also had to deal with the crank calls from people claiming that they had committed the murders, that aliens had experimented on the victims, or that divine retribution had fallen on four sinners. Otherwise, the room was quiet.

Brett took advantage of the lull to visit Sue Kilbracken in her laboratory. She was peering into a microscope on a clean white worktop. In front of her, there were long rows of shelves containing specimen jars, pickled organisms, reagent bottles and countless insects pinned in racks. It looked grotesque, like a chamber of miniature horrors.

Sue looked up at him and smiled. She seemed delighted to entertain the young and handsome officer in her parlour. Brightly she said, "Ah, Brett. You've come at a good time. I've just got something for you. Your luck's in today. On here," she reported, indicating the slide, "I have the pupal cases of *Phormia terraenovae*. It's a rare fly and only on the wing in May. The specimens came from Victim Number One so he must have died last May. Thirteen months ago, for sure."

Brett congratulated her. "Good work," he uttered. "That's useful."

"I've been checking out the insects in the soil under the bodies – the ones that were covered with branches. It gives me a handle on how long those victims have been lying there. The answer is, they've been in those positions since they were killed. That means they were killed on the spot or dumped there soon afterwards."

"They weren't murdered, left somewhere for quite a while, and then put in the wood?"

"No. Certainly not."

"How about the white substance on Victim Number Four?" Brett enquired.

"No result yet. Gone for chemical and microbiological analysis. They'll report tomorrow, all being well." Sue paused and then added, "The age of the maggots on him suggests a date of death eleven days before discovery, even if the corpse was a bit more bedraggled than you'd expect after that time."

"OK. Thanks," Brett responded. With a grin, he added, "That uncertainty's still the fly in the ointment, though." When Sue screwed up her face and let out a theatrical groan, Brett said, "Sorry. Can you fax your results through to me so I've got them on paper?"

"I'll do better than that. I'm networked to your computers so I'll E-mail you a document with all my findings this afternoon."

"Fine. Thanks a lot." Brett hesitated before continuing, "Just one more thing, Sue. Pure curiosity. Why do you do it – studying insects? It intrigues me."

Sue laughed. "Because they're fun. Do you know how many insects there are on the planet?"

"Not a clue."

"Neither does anyone else, but there are perhaps three million living species. That outnumbers all other plant and animal groups. The number of mammalian species is insignificant in comparison. Forget mammals! Insects are so varied and intricate. Some are amazingly organized and full of community spirit. Terrific creatures. Entertaining little beasties."

Brett smiled. "The bee's knees," he said.

"Exactly," Sue rejoined, chuckling. "Everyone should love them."

"You'd have a hard time persuading a lot of people."

"True. Even if the living are sceptical about the beauty of insects, at least the dead don't deny them their right to recycle the elements. *And* they're useful for police work."

"So I'm discovering," Brett agreed. "I guess I wouldn't mind becoming insect fodder – just another link in the food chain – if it helped catch my killer." He shuddered at the thought. "Anyway," he said, "I'd better get going. You'll let me know as soon as you've identified the white stuff, won't you?"

Sue was captivated by his charm. "Sure will," she replied, obligingly.

The next day, shortly after Brett and Greg returned with more names, addresses and dates obtained from owners of holiday homes, Sue's final bulletin arrived at Brett's computer terminal. She reported that, as Brett suspected all along, the corpse of Victim Number Four had been infiltrated by a white fungus while buried in the ground.

Immediately, Brett was on the phone to Sue. When she answered, he thanked her for her help and asked, "This fungus, what effect would it have on your estimate of the time of death?"

Sue exhaled as she thought. "None, as far as I can see. I don't see why it should. Do you?"

"No. Not really," Brett replied. "I'm just aware that the body looked older than eleven days. Perhaps we're overlooking something. I've got a nagging feeling I know something relevant but I can't remember what. I need to think about it – or do a spot of library work." He paused and then said, "I'd also like to give some to a specialist I know up the road at the university. My old tutor. Is that OK with you? Can you send over a small sample of the fungus?"

"No problem," Sue replied, trying to be helpful. "I'll get that organized straightaway."

"Thanks."

When Brett briefed John, his commanding officer was unimpressed. Tersely, he asked, "So how does this fungus advance the investigation?"

"It doesn't," Brett admitted honestly. "But I'd like to check something out in a decent science library. My old university will let me use theirs."

"Library work?" John snapped. "Doesn't sound like something detective inspectors should be doing. Sounds like after-hours work. Something you do in your own time – such as it is."

"OK," Brett agreed. "I'll go tonight."

He didn't get to the library after all. That evening, he found himself driving to Macclesfield with John Macfarlane on a more pressing engagement. Two promising leads had emerged and they had decided to chase one immediately.

The computer had thrown up a couple of interesting coincidences. Two people who owned new silver Mercedes-Benz cars had been visiting Edale when some or all of the murders had been committed. Their names had been plucked out of the databases of car owners and visitors. Without comment, Liz handed the details over to Brett. She said nothing, but her expression was eloquent enough. She knew that one of the names would mean trouble for the team.

Brett glanced first at the computer's discovery and then at Liz. Frowning, he declared, "I'll take this to John."

"Good idea," Liz agreed.

In his turn, Big John read the slip of paper with a scowl on his face and then asked Brett to come into his office. He closed the door and tapped the print-out. "This is not as awkward as it seems," he remarked. "We don't have to investigate one of these people."

The troublesome name that the computer had selected was that of Detective Chief Superintendent Keith Johnstone. He had made weekend trips to the hotel in Edale on three occasions. He had reserved a double room for the May Day weekend the previous year, the New Year break, and the early Easter holiday that fell at the end of March.

"Why not?" Brett asked.

"Because he hasn't been in Edale in the last couple of weeks," John replied.

"Not as far as we know," Brett argued. "But what if Victim Number Four is older than entomology suggests?"

"Do you have any evidence that he is?"

"No. Not really," Brett confessed.

"So, Keith Johnstone isn't on our hit list then."

Brett shook his head slowly, clearly unconvinced. "I wanted to follow up anyone who hit two out of our three time frames."

"And I've just overruled you," Big John boomed. He had been in the game a long time and acted as if he could smell criminals. "I know Keith," he said, "and he's not our man. Besides, if you want to get on in this game you don't investigate your superior officers on suspicion of multiple murder. You trust high-ranking colleagues implicitly. Clear?"

Brett could not bring himself to agree. He just grunted. His scientific training and his instinct were being assaulted by John's edict. He had set clear criteria and Keith Johnstone had fulfilled them. He should be investigated. The fact that he was the Chief Superintendent had nothing to do with it, as far as Brett was concerned. It was an irrelevant fact. To Brett, a suspect was a suspect, irrespective of his standing. There was circumstantial evidence against him so the Chief *could* be guilty of the murders. It was only a theory – not even a likely one – but the scientific method now required Brett to test the theory, looking for facts that would disprove it and so eliminate the suspect. Detective Superintendent John Macfarlane had denied him that opportunity and so the theory remained unchallenged. In Brett's mind, Keith Johnstone remained a suspect. Brett also noted that the Detective Superintendent had booked a double room. If he took someone with him, there was a second suspect. A second dormant theory. The only contradictory fact that Big John had offered was that the Chief and his unknown companion had not been booked into a hotel in the past few days. Brett was not persuaded. A murder did not necessarily need an overnight stay and there was some lingering doubt about the time of death of Victim Number Four. Even so, Brett was forced to shelve that part of the investigation.

Instead, with John, he'd considered the second name on the list: Mr Andrew Smith of Macclesfield. Andrew Smith had stayed overnight in the same hotel, but on Wednesdays in May last year, March earlier this year and thirteen days ago. "Let's go and see what brand of cigarettes he smokes," John had suggested.

And so, instead of researching an idea in the library, Brett was driving Big John over the Pennines via the steep, bleak but attractive Winnats Pass.

As they cruised down the long, gentle descent towards Macclesfield, John said, "I want you to take the lead in this interview. After all, he's your suspect."

Brett felt like replying, "He's *one* of my suspects," but he decided not to push his luck. "OK," he answered.

"It doesn't mean I won't ask some questions – I'm sure I will – but I want to watch him. See how he reacts to what you say first."

"Fair enough," Brett said, happy to take centre stage for a while. He realized that Big John would be watching his performance as well. He knew that his commanding officer was assessing him constantly and critically. At the end of the investigation, John would write a report on him.

Andrew Smith turned out to be an accountant, in his late thirties, who smelt of money. He wore an expensive suit and lived in an expensive house. He was shorter than Brett, not quite as broad in the shoulders, but still fit. Brett and John interviewed him in his smart, pretentious lounge in the presence of his wife, Angela.

"We'd like to talk to you in connection with a current inquiry..."

Interrupting, the accountant asked, "Into what?"

"The deaths of four people in Edale."

"Do you mean murder?" he snapped.

"Yes."

There was an audible intake of breath from Angela.

Brashly, Andrew Smith asked, "What's it got to do with me?"

"Probably nothing," Brett answered. "But you were in the locality at the time of the murders and you may have seen something that could help our inquiries. Can you start by telling us why you go to Edale fairly regularly?"

"I have business meetings there. Mainly I take potential clients. Treat them to a good afternoon and evening. The mixture of business and pleasure, fresh air and brainstorming seems to impress them."

"So what do you do for the business part of the day?" Brett queried. "Hire a conference room in the hotel?"

Mr Smith hesitated. "Er ... there *is* a conference room but I've never needed to book it. It's always been free to use."

Even Brett could detect that the accountant was lying. The pause gave him away. Besides, he'd been trapped by Brett's cunning question. If he'd said that he had reserved the meeting room, he knew that Brett could easily check with the hotel staff and discover the deception. To avoid being exposed straightaway, he'd fabricated an unlikely answer. It was inconceivable that a businessman like Mr Smith would fail to book a room that he needed to bewitch a client. If it had not been available, he would have lost face in front of a potential punter. Mr Smith would have planned ahead meticulously. Brett did not believe for a moment that such meetings had taken place.

"Can you give me the names of the people you took there last May, in March, and a week last Wednesday?" asked Brett.

Mr Smith's face crumpled. "This sounds like an interrogation. Don't you believe me?" he cried. "I thought I was assisting your investigation, not under suspicion myself."

"You *are* helping us," Brett insisted. "As the incidents took place on each of those occasions, it follows that we'd like to talk to your contacts who were there at the same time. They may have seen something significant as well. So, who are they?"

"I don't know off the top of my head," Mr Smith answered. "You'd need to catch me in the office so I could consult my appointments book."

"You can't even recall last week's client?" Brett asked.

"I see a lot of people in my line of business," Andrew replied. "No. I can't remember."

"OK," Brett relented. He had discovered that the man had not been in Edale for business so he did not need to persist with that line of questioning. "When you were there on those three occasions, did you hear any gunfire?"

Mr Smith shrugged. "I don't think so. No."

"Are you familiar at all with the sound of gunshots?"

"No." Mr Smith paused and, with a grin, added, "Only from the telly."

"You don't fire guns yourself, then?"

"No. Never."

"When you go to Edale," Brett enquired, "do you go on your own?"

"Yes."

"You don't take your wife?" he queried, glancing at Mrs Smith, who looked decidedly uncomfortable with his current angle.

"No, purely business, I'm afraid," Andrew Smith said, loosening his floral tie and undoing the top button on his shirt.

"I believe you smoke," Brett observed, glancing at the ashtray on the coffee table. "What brand?"

"Benson and Hedges," he answered. "What possible use is that to your inquiries?"

Ignoring the question, Brett asked Angela Smith, "Do you smoke as well?"

Before Mr Smith could interrupt and protect his wife, she winced and mumbled, "No."

"Look," Mr Smith exclaimed. "This has gone far enough. It's one thing to question me but another to have a go at Angela as well. I've already told you she didn't come to Edale. This can't have anything to do with her."

"No, not directly, but I'm assuming that your wife goes in the car sometimes. If something from the car had been left in Edale, it could belong to you *or* your wife."

For the first time, John interceded. "I shouldn't put upon you, Mrs Smith, but I'm parched after the long journey. Is there any chance of a cup of tea or am I inconveniencing you too much?"

Angela rose, asked the other two if they would also like a drink, and then retreated.

As soon as the door closed behind her, John said quietly but incisively, "Any reasonable person would come to an obvious conclusion at this stage, Mr Smith. Detective Inspector Lawless was skirting round the point rather than getting there for fear of embarrassing your wife. Can we agree that you sometimes take to Edale a woman who is not your wife, and who smokes Silk Cut? Further, is it reasonable to propose that you parked your Mercedes off the road, scraping it a little in the process, and emptied the ashtray because you didn't want to drive home with cigarette stubs bearing incriminating lipstick stains?"

At first speechless, Andrew Smith stared at John. Then he hung his head. "Yes," he whispered, glancing towards the closed door to the kitchen.

"Right. Now we're getting somewhere. Let's carry on." By saying nothing more, effectively he handed the interview back to Brett.

"We'll need her name," Brett said quietly, almost apologetically.

"I can't give you that," replied Mr Smith.

"So, she's married," Brett deduced. "But we have to speak to her to corroborate your story. We'll be very discreet, I assure you."

"Sorry," Andrew murmured.

"It's a simple choice," John interjected to apply more pressure. "Either you continue to protect her, unnecessarily, and come under considerable suspicion of murder, or you co-operate and hopefully she clears your name."

Andrew Smith sighed but still muttered, "No."

"Well," Brett put in, "we'll simply have to trace her through her hotel reservations, concurrent with yours, no doubt."

"You won't find that easy," the accountant

growled almost boastfully. "She never uses her real name. A different name each time."

The kitchen door opened and Angela Smith walked in stiffly with a tray. Just about under control, but like a bomb on a short fuse, she announced, "It's more than likely to be his solicitor, Mrs Julie Penny."

Andrew looked at his wife with his mouth open. He cried, "What...? How...?"

She slammed down the tray and snapped, "Even infidelity's better than murder." Maintaining her dignity, she strode from the room.

After a few seconds of stunned silence, Big John levered himself out of the chair and proclaimed, "Thank you for your help, Mr Smith. I think we'd better pass on the tea, after all. You seem to have some sorting out to do here."

Brett followed his boss out of the house.

Back in the car, Brett let out a long breath as if dejected. "Don't you just love interfering in other people's domestic lives?"

"You're too sensitive," John told him. "Remember you're hunting a serial killer. Sometimes you have to tread on people's toes – if not trample all over them. Besides, it's no bad thing to have it out in the open. Maybe they can start to work something out now."

"Maybe the local force will be called out to his murder tonight," Brett replied.

John shook his head and then laughed. "No chance. His wife isn't the type. Anyway, good job you didn't want an early night tonight. Let's go and find this Julie Penny. See if we can get that discreet interview you promised. But don't forget *she's* a suspect as well, now."

Using the Yellow Pages, they found a number for Penny, Gallup and Tomlinson Solicitors. At night, there was no one in the office but the answerphone gave an emergency number. That number was the same as that for S D Penny of 14 Cedar Way in the telephone directory.

It turned out that Julie Penny's husband, Stephen, was away so Brett and John were able to talk to her freely. When Brett introduced himself, she laughed. Interrupting him, she said, "We've got something in common already. Inappropriate names. People say solicitors should be called 'an arm and a leg', not Penny. I dread to think what they say about a police officer called Lawless."

"I bet you'd argue that a conspicuous name didn't stop you being a good solicitor," Brett rejoined with a significant glance at his commanding officer.

"I'd say it helps," Julie replied, turning on her charm.

She was more glamorous than Angela Smith. She was in her thirties, tall, elegant and confident. Her eyebrows rose when Brett informed her which case he was investigating, and her mood changed as he began the interview with the subject of her relationship with Andrew Smith. "Who told you about that?" she asked aggressively. "Surely not Andrew."

"No," Brett replied. "He was far too chivalrous.

Actually, it was his wife." He paused for the implication to sink in.

Julie's face first expressed surprise, then shock, followed by annoyance. "Damn. That particular apple cart has been well and truly upset." She took a cigarette from the packet on the occasional table, lit up, and inhaled deeply.

"We have no wish to pry into your relationship," Brett commented, "but we do need to verify your trips to Edale with Mr Smith."

As Brett mentioned the date of each visit she nodded and, in a resigned tone, murmured, "Yes." Smoke swirled from her mouth with each confirmation.

"Why did you use a false name every time?"

"Isn't it obvious? I have an inquisitive husband."

"OK," Brett replied. "Do you ever go to Edale without Mr Smith?"

Mrs Penny answered, "Yes. Occasional day trips. At the start of each year, I have to see a client there. Not particularly onerous but the first visits, many years ago, made me enamoured of the area." She pointed to a framed sketch hanging on the wall behind her. A dark, atmospheric drawing of a rocky outcrop in the High Peaks. "It's gorgeous," she purred.

"OK. Now, these weekends with Mr Smith," Brett began delicately, "what did you do on each of those occasions, other than be together, perhaps, in the hotel?"

"That's a very impertinent question!"

"But necessary," Brett added. "For example, did you go walking in the hills?"

"Once or twice."

"Whereabouts?"

"Look," the solicitor snapped. "This is preposterous." Her indignation showed itself as an inability to take his inquiries seriously. "You cannot possibly link me with a series of deaths just because I was nearby at the time! It's laughable. I'm a solicitor. If the murders occurred in the middle of Macclesfield, you wouldn't interview everyone in Macclesfield at the time."

"With all due respect," Brett retorted, "Edale is not Macclesfield. Besides, I didn't imply that your presence at the time of the murders made you a suspect. It makes you a potential witness." He extracted a map and insisted, "Can you locate any walks you may have taken?"

Reluctantly, she traced three paths with a nicotine-stained finger. None of them went close to the wood where the bodies lay.

Still silent, John Macfarlane watched the interchange between his new assistant and the new suspect.

"How about here?" Brett prompted. "Not far from the camp site. Did you ever walk or drive near here?"

"We didn't walk there but we must have driven along that road."

"Did you ever stop?"

Julie paused, thinking about his question. "Yes. We may have done so last time."

"For what purpose?"

She scowled at him. "What do you think? We ... er ... smoked a last cigarette together."

Brett did not have to check the brand. There was a packet of Silk Cut on the table.

"When would that be?"

"On the Thursday morning. About ten, I guess."

"Did you see anything unusual while parked there?"

Julie shrugged. "No. Absolutely not."

John and Brett left, not with proof of the innocence of the accountant and his solicitor, but at least with a consistent story. Of course, Smith and Penny could have agreed on the alibi beforehand. They could be telling the same lie. They could both be guilty.

"What did you think of her?" John asked on the way back to Sheffield. "Is *she* the type that kills?"

Brett wasn't sure. "Hard to tell. But you said yourself, serial killers are almost always male."

"Yes," the experienced detective agreed, "but I'm always prepared to make an exception. I thought you would've found out more about her trips if you'd probed harder. Still, as a lawyer, she'd be a tough nut for you." Changing tack before Brett could respond, he asked, "And what about Andrew Smith?"

"More of a possibility," Brett estimated.

"You've got to be joking. Behind his bravado, I detected a real wimp. Believe me, if it's one of those two, it's Mrs Julie Penny. Sweet one minute and spitting venom the next." Big John paused before adding, "Right now, though, I'm in serious need of a pie and a pint or two. Let's stop at the next pub. You're driving so you'll have to make do with the pie."

First thing in the morning, Brett went to see Tony Rudd, the Chief Forensic Pathologist. When Tony handed over his written report, swollen with graphic detail, Brett requested, "Just give me the edited highlights."

"Right you are. First, all the deceased. Eye socket and nose measurements suggest Caucasian. Not an entirely reliable test but the skin of Victim Number Four was once white. None had fractures or deformities. Cause of death – pretty obvious. Probably point three eight calibre, definitely placed against the side of the head. Now, Victim Number One. Degree of epiphyseal ossification suggests seventeen years of age. Time of death – at least a year ago. Quite athletic build. Measurements are all in the report." He spoke rapidly, as if he had another job waiting, and fired off bursts of facts like an automatic pistol. "The bullet and gas pressure cracked the skull. Interesting that the skeletal structure of the left arm was more developed than the right."

"What does that mean?" Brett queried. "That he was left-handed?"

"Probably. More than that, though. For some reason the left arm was exercised to a considerable extent."

"Any ideas?"

"I've seen it before with people who need particular strength on one side. Brick layers who always lift bricks with the same arm. That sort of thing."

"I see," Brett muttered thoughtfully.

"Victim Number Two," Tony continued in the same staccato fashion. "Female. Seventeen or eighteen. The bones of the pelvis indicate recent childbirth. Genetics found no decent DNA, so no maternity test possible."

"But Victim Number Three's likely to be her baby," Brett guessed.

"Young mother and son. It's logical but there's no evidence either way."

"If the father's out there somewhere – if he's not among the dead – I wouldn't mind talking to him," Brett remarked wistfully.

Keen to move on, Tony added, "Just one other oddity about Victim Number Two. There was a nick out of the left tibia, ten centimetres above the ankle."

"Her shinbone." Brett pondered on it. "What caused it? Any idea?"

"A sharp instrument. A knife. Quite a severe wound. Severely hacked."

"It wasn't post-mortem damage? A predator scratching at her remains, for example."

"No." The pathologist was certain. "The cut's too straight and deep for post-mortem injury. On top of that, the lips of the cut tell me it was inflicted on live bone."

"But it wasn't a fatal wound?" Brett queried.

Tony grimaced at him. "Not compared with a bullet through the head. No. Nasty cut. Lots of blood but no real problem. You should be asking me the obvious question. The direction of the hacking action."

Brett muttered, "OK. Go on. Tell me."

"Upward," he stated bluntly, enjoying watching Brett's puzzled face.

"Upward? And yet it was struck only a few centimetres from the ground. That's some low blow!"

"Yes. The blade was coming up slightly when it hit the leg, perhaps twenty centimetres from the ground. That's if the subject was standing at the time."

"You're proposing she wasn't upright when she received the wound?"

"I'm giving you the facts. I'm not proposing any-thing. But it *is* hard to strike upwards at a target twenty centimetres from the ground. If the victim were lying on her back, or dangling upside down, it might make more sense. Anyway, I can't tell you any more."

"All right," Brett replied. "Thanks. Victim Number Three?" He shivered as he thought of the murdered child.

"Male. Probably three weeks old. Killed three months ago or thereabouts – the same as Victim Number Two. Nothing else of note." Tony continued with his findings, hardly drawing breath. "Victim Number Four. Male. Even less epiphyseal ossification. Probably fifteen or sixteen. Discrepancy with entomology – several body cavities had burst and tissues liquefied, indicating death occurred weeks, if not months, ago."

"Months!"

"No more than six."

"You've heard the insect evidence?" asked Brett, still shocked by his revelation.

"Yes," Tony replied. "And I know Sue Kilbracken. She's good. I can't explain the difference. I just report my findings. Maggots or not, my opinion is that the body's been buried for a while. I prefer to stick to the facts but if you want speculation, remember the first three or four months of the year were very cold. Low temperatures slow everything down, including decay. Just under the surface, Victim Number Four could have been virtually frozen till the weather picked up. Then a few weeks of decay, followed by the foxes. The body *could* be six months old. But I don't know what the maggots were playing at. They shouldn't have been there."

Brett sighed and shook his head. "That's a pain."

"It's the type of result that keeps police officers in work," Tony mused. "In forensics, we don't have all the answers. If we did, we wouldn't need you lot on the streets. We'd solve all the crimes for you."

"I guess so," Brett admitted, managing a wry smile. Changing the subject, he enquired, "Any chance of being able to say if the bodies were moved after they died?"

"Usually," Tony answered, "but not in this case. Decomposition of the corpses put paid to any hypostasis."

"Pity," Brett mumbled to himself.

The day did not improve. The computer found lots of matches with known missing persons but, when the improved accuracy of the victims' details was taken into account, each correlation broke down. The missing teenager would have teeth with fillings, healed broken bones, or would be the wrong height. Then, one by one, the teams that had been saturating the area with the description of Victim Number Four reported that no one had recognized him. They had come across a few leads but each ended when boys, somewhat similar to Victim Number Four, had been found alive and kicking. Two football players in a youth team based in Castleton had reported that an unknown boy who used to turn up from nowhere and watch their matches had suddenly stopped making his regular appearances, but that was some time ago – at the height of the football season. It didn't correspond with the killing of Victim Number Four. Frustrated, all eight officers had returned empty-handed to base camp.

Over a coffee, John Macfarlane and Brett held a briefing to double-check that the team had covered the whole region. Brett found himself sitting next to the pair that had just returned from the smallest speck on the Edale map – Upper Needless. "Stuck out in the middle of nowhere," they told him. "No one seems to have heard of it."

"I have," Brett said. "I heard a lad swearing at people from Upper Needless."

"The two of you must be the only ones."

"What's it like?" asked Brett.

"It's a sort of commune, I suppose. Remote. Quiet. Old-fashioned. The sort of place where you can't sneeze without the whole village knowing you've got a cold. The sort of place you could nuke from the face of the earth and no one else would notice."

"And they haven't got any missing youngsters?"

"No. We asked the few people we could see. They didn't know anything."

The dead were not readily yielding their secrets. Without identities and without a pattern to the murders, the detectives were working in a vacuum.

"We've lost our way as far as the identities are

concerned," Big John asserted. "Time to wheel in the big guns. Facial reconstruction."

"Really?" Brett murmured. "I thought that was just done in films and crime novels."

"No," John assured him. "It can be done. But forget cleaning the skull by getting beetles to eat the residual flesh, and using plasticine and sculpture. It's all done in minutes by computer now. It can give us likenesses – almost photographs – of our victims to hawk around."

"It actually works, building a face from a skull?" Brett queried.

"You're my forensic supremo – or supposed to be. Get down there and find out from the experts how good it is."

In the anatomy department, Brett was directed to a medical illustrator called Lauren. She was introverted, looked much younger than her twenty-eight years, and was forever fiddling with her long mousy hair and adjusting the position of her glasses on her nose. She could work miracles on a computer while simultaneously claiming that the techniques at her disposal were simply not up to the job. She had started her career with a plastic surgeon, forecasting the results of cosmetic surgery, but had soon become disillusioned. She had hoped to help those who suffered deformities but mostly found herself pampering the vanity of those who were not satisfied with the bone structure that nature had given them and had the money to change it. She joined the forensic-science department, where she exploited her expertise to predict the facial appearance of long-lost people from their childhood photographs, and mapped the anatomical landmarks of unearthed skulls on to pictures of missing persons to confirm identities. She had been known to be amazingly accurate. Her methods had shot to prominence two years previously when she produced age-advanced portraits of two abducted brothers. She based her calculations on photographs taken eight years earlier, just before they had been snatched. Within fifteen minutes of her pictures appearing on national television, teachers and neighbours called the police, identifying the boys in Birmingham. They looked exactly like Lauren's age-advanced pictures. Their father was arrested for abduction and the brothers were reunited with their mother.

After Brett had explained his problem, she told him, "The trouble is, a face is defined by the size and shape of fourteen key bones and over one hundred muscles. Sounds like three of your victims lost most of that information some time ago."

"Yes, but we have their skulls, albeit with extra holes and cracks in them."

"Yes, yes," Lauren grumbled, "but the real individuality of a face – like the eyes, facial hair and lips – are hardly dependent on the bone structure underneath."

Still keen to secure her services, he commented, "The lads were adolescents. You could assume they didn't have much in the way of facial hair."

"I suppose I could do a job on your Victim Number Four. The others I could attempt, but there'll be too much speculation."

"Fair enough. We'd still be interested. It's better than nothing."

"Is it? It's worse if it misleads," she suggested pessimistically.

"I'm sure you won't be that far wide of the mark."

Avoiding eye contact with Brett, she concluded, "Well, I'll give it a go, if you insist. First, get me a copy of the pathologist's notes and photographs, and fix me up with a visit to the morgue. Then I'll get on to it – for what it's worth."

Keith regarded the most trusted member of his staff across his formidable and tidy desk. "I see," he muttered. "That's ... unfortunate."

"Yes," Big John agreed. "I thought I'd better tell you in case he breaks rank and tries to pester or embarrass you. You know how obsessive youngsters can get about investigations when they begin to take responsibility."

"Yes, I know," Keith responded. "Let's talk frankly, though." With an ironic smile, he said, "Really, you'd approve if he did investigate me. Secretly, you'd applaud such initiative."

John would not admit it. He said, "But it doesn't do much for loyalty and trust. What would you do if he stepped out of line?"

"I thought you didn't care about such whipper-snappers," Keith taunted him.

"For better or worse, he's part of my team. Someone was most insistent that he should be! Now he is, I expect a lot of work from him, and in return he deserves my protection."

"OK, John. I hear what you're saying. But if he pursues me at all, from what you've told me, he'd be disobeying a direct order from you – his commanding officer. He'd have to be disciplined for any such breach. Do you hear what *I'm* saying? Lawless doesn't mean being a law unto himself."

"All right," John replied. "Let's hope it doesn't come to that. But I've warned you. He's an enthusiastic police officer. Already, I see he's committed and opinionated. He thinks he's got a lead and he wants to follow it up. He could become a loose cannon."

"Perhaps you'd better teach him about respect as well – before he gets into hot water."

John shrugged. "I can try, but it's not my strongest point."

Before John could get out of the door, Keith asked, "By the way, John, this Edale case – any chance you'll need to carry firearms at some point?"

John frowned. "I hope not, but given what we're chasing, it's possible. Why?"

"Just planning ahead," Keith said evasively. "Diana needs to field test a new gun. I'm thinking you might be the man to do it."

Big John grimaced again. "You know me. I don't like guns, whatever the shape and size. I'd rather not carry anything. But if I do, it doesn't make any difference to me what it is."

"OK," Keith concluded. "I'll give it some thought."

It seemed that several people were addicted to the Vale of Edale. Their names appeared over and over again on lists of visitors to the area. They were hiking enthusiasts and they spent every available weekend tramping the Pennine Way. Any one of them could also be addicted to murder. John and Brett dispatched teams to interview some of the suspects and spent the rest of the day chasing the remainder themselves. It was a fruitless exercise. The people that they talked to in Sheffield, Rotherham, Stockport and Chesterfield were perfectly normal and innocent.

After they'd finished the circus of interviews at 8.45pm, John instructed Brett to drop him off at his local pub. Brett was amazed by his appetite for beer. His liver must be taking a hammering. During a serious case like this one, the stomach took a hammering as well. Food had become an endless succession of pies, greasy sausage and chips, sand-wiches and kebabs from a range of disreputable takeaways. Brett was grateful that driving gave him an excuse for avoiding the alcoholic binges. He was determined not to follow in Big John's unwholesome footsteps. Tonight, he promised himself a decent, healthy meal. But before he cooked, he paid a visit to his old tutor at the university.

Professor Derek Jacob was a shrewd chemist, adept at talking money out of the chemical industry to fund his burgeoning research. Dressed in a brilliant white lab coat, the lecturer was working late, supervising a laboratory of part-time students. He seemed able to keep track of all of the projects – measuring organic acids in urine, aspirin in tablets, nicotine in cigarettes – and still have a moment to sit at a desk working on his latest application for funds. There was not a single test-tube in sight. Instead, the lab was teeming with bench-top instruments and computers.

He rose and held out his hand fondly to Brett. "Well, well, well. Brett Lawless! Have you changed your mind? Come to your senses? You want a research post after all? A law-less future."

Shaking his head, Brett laughed and muttered, "No."

"I thought not. You're here for a reason, though. Don't tell me you're wanting to recruit me to the police force!"

"Sort of," Brett replied. "I might need your expertise at biochemical analysis."

"No problem," the chemist responded smartly. "I

can use the cash the police force will heap on me for being a consultant. Maybe my research students will be able to afford to eat tonight after all."

Brett continued the banter. "You'll be lucky. We're as strapped for cash as you are. Besides, I only want a CAS online search. Any chance?"

Derek sighed. "Is that all? I thought you were going to give me something to get my teeth into. Thought I was going to solve the crime of the century for you." He thrived on challenges.

"You never know," Brett said. "Depends what the literature search throws up."

"Nip down the corridor, then. My office is open and the computer's on. Do you remember how to get into the system? Do you remember the departmental password?"

"It was drummed into me like my own phone number. I reckon I'll remember it when I'm ninety."

Derek's office had not improved. Every surface, every shelf and table was littered with a bewildering array of papers. In the corner of one desk there was a small collection of coffee-stained mugs that had not seen soapy water for a considerable time. The computer emerged from the disorder like a ship on the sea. Brett shifted a pile of books from a chair, settled himself in front of the PC and called the Chemical Abstracts Service. Once connected to the remote database, he searched for information using the terms that he had worked out during the day. He knew that flies were attracted to rotting flesh by its stench and he wanted to discover more. He used the terms, fly, *Phormia*, attractant, carrion, carcass and death. The number of chemical articles on flies – more than twenty-two thousand of them – was soon whittled down to a manageable number when he cross-referenced each hit with the other terms. After a few minutes, he was left with the details of nine articles. While he waited for a printout, he skimmed through the nine abstracts on screen. "The odour trail of carrion is the major stimulus for invasion and egg-laying by *Phormia*." An extract of the next paper, published as early as 1962 in the *Journal of Insect Physiology*, seemed to promise him what he wanted. "Olfactory receptors on the antennae respond to aldehydes, alcohols and a number of other natural products. Firing of sense organs on the anal leaflet and ovipositor appear to elicit egg-laying behaviour."

He grinned, logged off and headed back to the lab. "I got what I wanted, thanks." He hesitated before adding, "I wonder if you could do a bit of work for me after all."

"You mean I *am* going to solve the crime of the century?" The professor was delighted.

"Something like that," Brett pronounced.

Behind Derek, a student working by the fume cupboard lit a cigarette that was attached to a length of rubber tubing and a pump. The tip glowed intensely while the contraption drew air rapidly through the cigarette, smoking it in a single manic drag. In a few seconds, there was nothing left but the filter tip. The machine had devoured the tobacco faster than a nervous chain-smoker, and trapped the nicotine for analysis.

From his jacket pocket Brett brought out the sample of dirty white powder, sealed inside a small plastic bag. "I'd be interested in what chemicals this fungus gives off."

Derek took the bag and held it up to the light. "Mmm. Not exactly generous but it's probably enough."

"Head-space analysis," Brett prompted. In a whisper, out of the hearing of the students, he explained the case to Derek.

"OK," Derek said. "Fascinating. You've got me hooked. I'll fit it in tomorrow. Get one of my research students to set it up for you. Since you left I've got a new GC/MS. A hundred times more sensitive than the one you once played with. You ought to come tomorrow and see it in action. You'll be impressed. Bet it'll make you crave for the old days!" As he walked to the door with his former student, he muttered, "I still don't understand how you could give up all this." He indicated the chemistry laboratory. "It's got far more juicy and exciting problems to solve than you'll ever get with the police."

"Out there," Brett replied, pointing beyond the entrance to the cloistered Chemistry Department, "there's a real world with real problems." He thanked Derek again and then strode back to his car.

The notion of an eight-hour working day and five-day working week was laughable during a serious case. Laying down the law was not a job that kept to a schedule. It was nearly ten o'clock by the time he got home. Too late to prepare the healthy meal that he had promised himself. Instead he microwaved some junk food and took it into the lounge, lit eerily by the aquarium lamp. In the corner of the room his only companions, the tropical fish, weaved and flashed. He ate the meal in front of the television news. Under the TV, the red light on his unused video recorder flashed *00:00 Sun* because he had not got around to setting the time. He forked the food distractedly, read the computer output from his literature search, and listened to the news at the same time. The Edale investigation had dropped down the billing. The report was phrased to give the impression that Detective Superintendent John Macfarlane was stumped and that the case was going nowhere. Brett murmured a curse. For a while, his mind turned to the one lead that he had been forbidden to follow. He tried to think of a means of exploring surreptitiously the Chief Superintendent's movements, but failed. It was not easy – and it was certainly dangerous. He also wondered if, in thirty years' time, he would be like Big John – his blood pressure as high as it would go, short of breath, pear-shaped, bloated with beer and fat-laden fast food, next in line for a heart attack. Clearing up after the snack, he vowed that he would not allow work to interfere with a healthy breakfast and morning run, no matter what it did to the rest of his day. And he would squeeze in as much sport as he could. He had no wish to join John in the queue for the cardiac unit.

After the bulletin had finished, Brett listened to the messages recorded by his telephone answering machine during the day. An old friend had called, suggesting that they meet for a drink at a time that had passed two hours ago. The coach of the rugby team informed him that he had missed the last two training sessions and, with irritation in his tone, queried Brett's dedication to the club. Finally, Brett recognized a chirpy female voice that made him cringe. "Hi, Brett! Diana here. Just to let you know I've swung it. I've got a real treat for you. Expect some good news tomorrow." Brett groaned at the enthusiasm of the Chief Firearms Technician. As if he hadn't got enough to worry about tomorrow without her mysterious scheme.

On Lauren's computer screen, the detached head of a teenage boy appeared like the afterglow of a lost spirit. Brett was reminded of his tropical fish. Floating so close, but occupying a different, ghostly world. Slowly, the head rotated. The screen had become a window to the dead. Neither Lauren nor Brett spoke. They were both saddened. He was a good-looking fresh-faced boy, about sixteen years old, brought back to uncanny life by a computer programme. As the facsimile continued to turn, it struck Brett that Victim Number Four did not have a lived-in face at all. It was as if he had been born at the age of sixteen. He had been resurrected cruelly without a personality, without even a name. Now that he had a face, it seemed heartless to deprive him of a name. But for a while at least, he had to remain a number in a police file. His forehead was bold but his eyebrows were not prominent. He had big eyes, a strong nose and conspicuous cheek bones. The ears were large but did not protrude in an ungainly way. His face tapered slightly and then cut off squarely at his broad jaw. He was neither smiling nor grimacing. It was a bland expression. Between his lips, there was a hint of uneven teeth. Lauren had not given his chin the stubble that would have added a couple of years to his demeanour.

Like a modern-day Frankenstein, Lauren remarked, "You could have whatever colour hair and whatever length you want. If you want people to concentrate on his face when trying to recognize him, I recommend this short fair hair and mundane style. If you add distinctive hair, experience shows everyone makes their judgement on the most distinctive feature – the hair. I suggest this neutral expression for the same reason. If people see a smiling face or a glum one, they only search their memories for a happy or morose boy. I've made his eyes a nondescript colour as well. People can see in them what colour they want."

Brett shrugged. "Sounds sensible enough."

"But don't forget," she warned. "This could be a long way off his real appearance. Maybe he wore glasses. Maybe his lips were thicker or thinner. Maybe he was covered with spots, warts, anything."

"I'll bear it in mind."

"What do I download for you?" Lauren asked. "The usual full face and both profiles?"

"Yes, please," Brett replied. "And what about the other two victims?"

"If Number Four's a long shot, the others are sheer conjecture." Lauren's fingers ran over her keyboard. Victim Number Four disappeared and a second face began to appear. The computer added layer on layer until the window provided a different view. This time a young woman's features hovered on screen, like a three-dimensional mask that hid a real person who had once had a real life. "One exception," Lauren reported. "The local birds did you a favour. By using some of Victim Number Two's hair in their nests, they've kept a record of it. I can be quite sure about the length and colour. Her face, though, is a different matter. But I've done what I can." She frowned, plainly dubious at the value of her own work.

"Thanks," Brett responded, deliberately using an upbeat tone. He had learnt that Lauren had a reputation for both accuracy and scepticism. He waited for the hard copy, three portraits of each adult victim, expressed his gratitude again, and then breezed back to the incident room. He got someone to photocopy the pictures while he called together the team and told them about the facial reconstructions.

Immediately, Greg muttered cynically, "I saw it done in a film a few years ago. The heads turned out to be spot on. Pure fiction. How accurate are they likely to be?"

Handing out the copies, Brett replied, "They're the best we've got. The face of Victim Number Four – the youngest – should be a pretty good likeness. The girl's hair is right; that we do know."

"So, we hit the road again, asking mainly if anyone saw Victim Number Four in the past month, say?" Greg enquired in a deliberate tone that was meant to sabotage Brett's earlier decision about the uncertain time of death.

Brett relented. He had to believe in the insect evidence until he had definite grounds for refuting it. Despite his misgivings, it was still the best theory. "Yes," he said. "That's the approach for the moment. Later today or tomorrow, I hope to bring you a better estimate of the timing. Now," he continued, subjecting himself to another day with Greg, "I want to come with you and cover the patch that includes Upper Needless. I once heard someone describe the villagers there as weirdos. I want to know why. The place sounds intriguing." He didn't mention that he was also intrigued by the Upper Needless woman he had encountered in Hope.

From a distance, Big John called to Brett, "That's OK, but I need you back here by 3.30. You and me, we're being hauled in to Firearms. Routine refresher for me. I don't know why you're getting dragged into it. But the message has come in from they-who-must-be-obeyed, even in the middle of a major investigation." He uttered this with disgust. "Make sure you get back on time," he concluded. With a glint in his eye, he added, "And remember to watch out for George Bottomley's sheep that have gone walkies."

Brett organized the rest of the team into pairs and assigned them to different areas of the vale. Clare Tilley was examining the pictures of the victims and shaking her head. "All right, Clare?" asked Brett.

"Yeah," she replied. "It's one thing dealing with skeletons but now I can see the victims as they were," she said, tapping the computer-generated images, "it really hurts. They're just ordinary kids. Thought I was getting immune to awful deeds but I was wrong. I'm not unshockable after all."

"If I were you," Brett remarked, "I'd stay that way. It'd be more of a tragedy if we all regarded this as normal. You should stay shockable."

Clare nodded and smiled faintly. "Guess so."

"Makes you wonder why there isn't a queue of irate parents at the door, demanding to know what happened to their kids, though," Greg put in.

"Good point," Brett acknowledged. "And the baby's father. Unless he's dead as well, why isn't he kicking up a fuss?"

"Maybe the fact that he isn't is good evidence that he's one of our bodies," Greg replied in a prickly tone, suggesting the answer was obvious. "Getting her pregnant could've been just about the last thing Victim Number One did."

"No wedding ring on the woman," Clare chipped in. "She was probably single. Perhaps the father's alive but doesn't know he's a father."

"Could be," Brett said. "Let's get going but keep all this in mind."

On his way to the door, Greg whispered to Mark, "I've cracked it. BSc stands for Brainy but Superfluous Cop!"

They both laughed aloud.

As he set out with Greg, Brett hoped that Clare had not got the impression that he was trying to avoid her. Next time, he decided he would make her his partner. For the moment he needed to work on his relationship with Greg. Brett believed that if he could win over Greg, he could win over them all.

Automatically, Brett got into the driver's seat and headed towards the Hathersage road. "Don't you want me to drive?" Greg checked.

"Why?" Brett asked. "Because you hold a lower rank? I don't believe in that sort of thing."

"Perhaps you don't trust me."

Brett laughed. "No. I trust you implicitly." Glancing at his partner, Brett said, "Let's sort this out right now. You've got a problem because you're more experienced but find yourself subordinate to me. You think that's unfair. Right?"

"To put it mildly, it's a source of aggravation," Greg replied.

"I can see that," Brett agreed. "It's understandable. But perhaps *you* should trust *me* as a colleague. I'm learning and you can help me – or make my life pretty miserable. It's up to you, but I think I can bring something to this investigation as well as learn from it. Believe me, I don't want your respect if I don't deserve it. All I want is to be given an opportunity to earn it. Not too much to ask, is it?"

Still hostile, Greg watched the passing countryside to avoid eye contact. "I suppose not," he muttered.

Brett guessed that he was not going to make any more progress with Greg and so he changed the subject. He talked about last season's football, grumbling at the league positions of both Wednesday and United. At first, Greg seemed surprised that someone who had been to university should be interested in football. He chipped in with his own observations on the two leaky defences and soon he was chatting animatedly. Gradually, he warmed to Brett.

Past Hope, the small road followed the railway line. After Brett had turned sharp right into the tiny road to Upper Needless, gone under the track for the third time and came into view of the remote hamlet, he stopped the car.

"What's wrong?" Greg enquired.

"Nothing," answered Brett. "But, tell me, what do you see?"

Greg shrugged irritably. "One deadly boring village. What else?"

"Perhaps I should ask what you don't see," Brett said. "No cars in the street. No telegraph poles."

"You're right," Greg murmured. "No phones. Heaven."

"And no aerials on the roofs. I doubt they're on cable, either," Brett quipped.

"I always suspected that heaven would be mind-numbingly dull."

"Oh, well. Let's get on with it." Brett pulled into the village and parked outside a grocery store.

When the police officers got out of the car, they felt like unwanted strangers riding into a frontier town. Curtains twitched and an old woman, sweeping her front path, leaned on her broom and stared icily at them.

Greg's eyebrows rose. "Charming," he muttered sarcastically.

"Just a tight-knit community," Brett rejoined. He always tried to avoid hasty criticism or condemnation. Pointing to the shop, he said, "Might as well start here. Good as anywhere."

When they strode into the shop, all activity ceased. They could have been standing in front of an oil painting. The middle-aged woman behind the counter froze. The girl who was probably her daughter dropped a bag of carrots and the male customer lost interest in his order. Instead, he stared at the police officers as if they were aliens. The shop was old-fashioned – a still life of a bygone age. It had none of the trappings of modern shopping. No electronic till. No display of brightly packaged confectionery to tempt the kids. In fact, there was nothing in the whole store for the sweet-toothed. It stocked only the essentials. Home-baked bread, vegetables, fruit, cheese. If Brett's mind had not been preoccupied with the murder case, he would have replenished his supply of groceries.

"Hello," he said brightly. "Nice day."

The woman nodded at him tentatively.

"Detective Inspector Lawless," he announced, "and Detective Sergeant Lenton."

"If you're police," the shopkeeper stammered, "you want to talk to Thomas Adamson, not me."

"Thomas Adamson?" Brett queried.

"At this time, he'll be in the hall or his house. The big one next to the hall. Up the road, on your left."

"Fine," Brett said. "We'll go and see him when we've asked you all a question, if you don't mind."

"We've already answered your questions."

"Yes. I know you had a visit from some of our colleagues, but now we want to show you something." He nodded to Greg, signifying that he should lay out the pictures on the counter. "This road's a dead end so I bet you don't get many tourists, but take a look at these faces and tell me if you've ever seen them before."

The woman made a token gesture by glancing towards the pictures and then shook her head firmly. The customer examined them more seriously but he came to the same conclusion. "Nope," he declared.

"The younger boy could have been round these parts a couple of weeks ago," Greg put in.

"Nope," the man repeated even more forcibly. "Definitely no one like that round here these past two weeks."

Brett studied the man as he delivered his verdict. As far as Brett could gather, he appeared to be telling the truth. The young woman kept her eyes averted and occupied herself by picking up the carrots. She was either very shy or unwilling to offer help. "What about you?" Brett prompted.

Reluctantly, she looked at the three faces in turn. "I don't know them."

"Sure?"

She nodded in response.

"OK," Brett said. "We'll go and find this Thomas. Who is he, exactly?"

"He's the village elder," the woman explained, obviously pleased that the police officers were about to leave.

"Right. The village elder. Thanks."

Outside, Greg sighed. "Phew! Weirdos, eh? I agree."

"Just isolated," Brett commented, still finding reason to exonerate them. He appreciated that intrusion by the police would be unwelcome and disturbing to such a closed community.

They strolled up the street, past the woman with the broom, past a small playing field with a makeshift and deserted tennis court, past sleepy cottages. The homes were old and solid, mostly made from local stone, and well maintained. Next to a small primary school, the village hall was a large wooden structure like an overgrown scout hut. Just beyond it, Thomas

Adamson's residence was a smart and imposing building with a beautifully tended garden. More like a mansion than a house. By its hedge was parked the old decrepit car that had stalled in Hope.

Brett banged on the door of the hall and walked straight in. He expected to see table-tennis and snooker tables but inside it was laid out like a church. There were rows of wooden chairs like pews, all facing away from the door. At the front, where in a real church there would be an altar and pulpit, there was a stage occupied by a long table and chairs facing Brett and Greg.

They expected Thomas Adamson to be a rickety old man but the elder was a fit, upright man, about forty-five years old. He was standing by the table, sorting piles of papers. As soon as Brett and Greg entered the hall, he came down from the stage to greet them. "Good morning," he pronounced. "Can I assume you're more policemen?"

"What makes you think that?" Brett replied.

Thomas smiled. "We don't see many outsiders here. It can't be a casual visit. And, if you don't mind me saying so, all you officers seem to go round in pairs."

"So do Jehovah's Witnesses," Greg countered.

"Do they?" Thomas said. "But I bet they're not big beefy chaps like you."

Getting down to business, Brett said, "We're still trying to establish the identity of three murder victims found only a mile or so from here. I believe you've already spoken to a couple of officers." Seeing Thomas nod, Brett continued, "We called in at the grocery shop but they were … a bit frosty, if you'll forgive me for saying so. They referred us to you."

"I apologize," Thomas said. "We keep ourselves to ourselves round here. Our social graces might be a bit rusty. Mrs Hevey and Jane are well-meaning, but not used to strangers. You may have noticed that we tend to shun the outside world. In Upper Needless there's only three concessions to the modern world. The car outside. I've got one of those new-fangled mobile telephones – I'm sure you use them all the time – just for essential communication. And radio. Several of us have radios so we can hear news of the atrocities being committed in the outside world – like your murders. It reminds us how lucky we are to be cut off from it. Anyway, enough of our excuses. What can I do for you, now you've found me?"

Greg produced the portraits of the dead. "We had these made up and we want to know if you recognize any of them." He pointed to Victim Number Four and remarked, "Especially this young lad. Could have been around these parts quite recently. Two or three weeks ago, perhaps?"

Thomas took a long hard look at the face. "No, I don't think so. A couple of weeks, you say. No, I haven't seen anyone like that."

Thomas was robust but not tall. He looked up at both Brett and Greg when he addressed them. Unlike the other villagers, he sought eye contact every time he spoke. His penetrating stare unnerved Brett. He was dressed casually but he held himself stiffly like an army officer.

"How about the girl?" asked Greg. "Take note of her hair."

"Mmm." Again, he took his time. "Pretty. I wish I knew her." He grinned.

A door to the right of the table on the platform opened and a young woman entered. She was wearing a long skirt down to the ground so she appeared to float across the stage. She stopped, embarrassed, when she saw that Thomas had company. She peered at Brett for a moment and then muttered, "Sorry."

Brett's pulse quickened. It was the dazzling passenger who had been in the car in Hope.

"It's all right, Zoe," Thomas said to her. "These gentlemen are police officers."

Brett smiled broadly at her and asked, "Did you get the car fixed all right?"

Startled, Thomas swivelled towards Brett. "You know my niece?" It was almost an accusation.

"We sort of met."

Zoe explained, "He was good enough to help when Grandfather's car broke down the other day. Stopped a man attacking us and pushed the car off the road." She smiled at Brett. Clearly, she regarded him as a champion.

Brett was pleased. She had remembered him.

"In that case," Thomas said, "I must thank you, er… You didn't say your name."

"Detective Inspector Brett Lawless."

"Thank you, Inspector Lawless. On behalf of Zoe and my father."

"No big deal," Brett responded. Addressing Zoe he said, "Can I just ask you to look at some pictures and tell me if you've seen any of these people before – maybe when you've been to Hope?"

Zoe looked at Thomas. She seemed unwilling but he nodded at her, denying her a means of escape. "Time to return the favour, Zoe," he said.

Gliding towards them tentatively, she cast another admiring glance at Brett. It made him realize that she was not wary of him but of the pictures of the dead. First, she examined Victim Number One. Ignoring Greg, she looked at Brett and said, "No. I don't know him."

"Try the next."

Greg held out the likeness of Victim Number Four and she gazed mournfully at the youthful face.

"The question is," Thomas put in, "have you seen him in the last two or three weeks?"

Zoe relaxed a little and answered. "No. Sorry."

Moving close to her, Brett said, "Just one more. A woman about your age – or a bit younger."

Zoe sighed audibly. When she next looked at Brett, there was moisture in her eyes. She apologized again, this time for the show of emotion. "Sorry. I…" She sniffed and whispered, "These are the ones who were killed, I suppose."

"I'm afraid so," Brett answered.

"It's horrible. Tragic. Poor things. But I can't help you."

"Sure?" Brett checked.

Zoe nodded. She wiped her eyes.

"My niece has been shocked by the murders. Understandably," Thomas interjected.

"Of course," Brett murmured considerately. "It's a very unpleasant business." He had the urge to put his hand on Zoe's arm but he resisted the temptation. He presumed that her uncle would not approve. "Thanks for your help, anyway," he said to her.

"Go and get on," Thomas advised her. "Take your mind off it. I'll see you later."

Relieved, Zoe turned and trudged back past the table. At the door, she glanced at Brett once more and then disappeared.

To Brett, the place seemed empty and miserable without her. Concealing his disappointment, he said, "Just one more question." He scanned the hall. "What on earth do you do in here?"

Thomas grinned. "We meet. We organize our work rotas. We celebrate. We worship."

"Worship?"

"We don't need all the trappings of a church to celebrate the simple life, following the ways of God."

"I see," Brett replied. "Well, thanks for your co-operation. Is there anyone else in the village who you think might be able to help us?"

Thomas exhaled as he thought about it. "I wouldn't have thought so. You can speak to any of us, of course, but I don't think you'll get anywhere. If Zoe and I, Mrs Hevey and Jane don't recognize them, I doubt anyone else here will. As I said, we keep ourselves to ourselves."

Walking back to the car, Greg passed his judgement on the people of Upper Needless. "That confirms it. *Religious* weirdos. A real backwater. And look," he said, pointing to a farm where a dog barked loudly, "No sign of tractors. We've gone back a century."

Greg was right. There were a few fields of crops and, beyond them, a flock of sheep and a small herd of cows. There was a horse-drawn plough but nothing mechanized. "Each to his own, Greg," Brett rejoined. "Perhaps they're just environmentalists. Organic farming."

"More to the point," Greg uttered, "was she lying?"

"Who? Zoe?"

"Of course."

Brett had mixed feelings. He didn't want to believe that she would lie to him, but she had reacted badly to the pictures of the victims. She might have been holding back or, as her uncle said, she might simply be sensitive to suffering. Brett wished that he was a surer judge of human nature. He could not keep out of his mind John Macfarlane's scathing criticism of him. He could almost hear the Superintendent say, "You've got to get inside their minds. You've got to understand people." Brett unlocked the car and got in. Acutely aware of his shortcomings, he confessed, "I'm not sure."

"To be frank," Greg retorted sourly, "*I* wasn't swayed by her looks. It was pretty obvious that you were. And you weren't exactly discouraging her interest in you. Anyway, I reckon she was hiding something."

Brett knew that his partner had a valid point. He did not try to argue. "Possibly," he admitted. "I may have to make a return journey and try again." To change the subject as he drove away, he said, "When we get back, I'd like you to dig up what you can on Upper Needless. You know, any reported disturbances, anyone getting themselves into trouble. That sort of thing."

"Yes," Greg replied. "I was going to."

Walking down the long drab corridor towards the underground firing range, Big John was in a bad mood. He grumbled, "Right in the middle of a case! I've got better things to do with my time than a refresher course."

"You're an Authorized Firearms Officer, then?" asked Brett.

"For my sins, yes. Over my time in the force, I've carried a gun once or twice each year. Maybe forty days in a total of thirty years. Fired one in anger perhaps four or five times. For that, I have compulsory regular practice." He groaned. "Keith asked if there was a chance that this case would require the issuing of firearms. What could I say? Of course it *could*. We're dealing with someone who kills with a gun. Next thing, you and I are both called in. I don't know why *you've* been summoned," he said, disapprovingly.

Brett did not want to admit that an enthusiastic Chief Firearms Technician was fixing it behind the scenes. Instead, he said, "In trials during training, I got the best marks on the firing range. Perhaps I caught someone's eye."

"So, you can shoot straight. But that's not all there is to it. It's bad enough having experienced officers like me being able to go around with guns, without having armed rookies as well. You might as well know I think it's inviting trouble." He paused before asking, "Are you eager to get involved with guns? Do they make you feel good? Excited?"

"No," Brett answered. "They worry me. I don't fancy pitched battles with bullets flying."

"Well, that's something," John conceded. He announced their arrival at the reception desk and then claimed, "Anyone who *wants* to become a Firearms Officer or marksman should be banned from becoming one straightaway."

Big John sat down heavily but Brett remained on his feet, shuffling tensely round the small room. They waited in silence for Diana.

She was a firearms expert and a member of the British Olympic shooting team, specializing in the small-bore sport pistol. About ten years older than Brett, she had short blonde hair, dressed smartly, and used a lot of make-up. Every year she developed a crush on a new male recruit. Her first problem was that while the novices passing through her hands remained about the same age each year, she grew older. Her second problem was that when she was flirting with the officers, she tried to pretend that the widening gap in age did not exist. As a result, she sometimes made a fool of herself. In making Brett her latest quarry, she was well wide of the mark. When she strode into the reception area, she beamed broadly at him. At once, John understood why Brett had been lured to the firing range.

Standing close to Brett so that her bare arm brushed lightly against him, she said, "Come on in. I've got a real treat for you two." She logged their names and time of arrival and then punched her security code into the lock on the door to the Firearms Department. Opening the door, she ushered them in like a protective matron, through the arch that bleeped boisterously if it detected a gun. The security device was there to ensure that no one walked out carrying an unauthorized firearm.

When they got to the range, Diana took them inside the same booth and presented both of them with a gun. With a mysterious grin on her face, she said, "Take a look at them and tell me what you think."

First, Big John broke the chamber and checked that his weapon was not loaded, then he weighed it in his hand. He shrugged. "Conventional thirty-eight revolver," he muttered uninterestedly.

When Diana turned to Brett, he agreed. "Same here."

"OK. Good. Now load up," she ordered. "Full chambers, please."

When they had completed the task, Diana handed out the ear defenders, and said, "Right. Take aim and fire once. John first."

After the muffled crack, Diana signalled that Brett should do the same.

Moving to the front of the booth, Brett allowed the gun to nestle into his hand. "Is this some sort of competition?" he shouted.

"No," Diana yelled back. "I don't even care if you miss altogether, but I bet you won't." She smiled endearingly at him.

As he took aim, he was reminded of a bowling alley. This time, though, the small target was suspended from the ceiling. The gun cracked, his arm jolted and he lowered the weapon.

Taking their lead from Diana, they removed their ear protectors. "Good shot," she congratulated Brett. Turning to John, she cooed, "He's my star pupil. First ever to score maximum marks. Anyway," she continued, "did you both feel comfortable?"

"As comfortable as it ever gets," John replied tersely.

"Yes," Brett concurred.

"Let me have them back for a moment," she commanded. Then, quite suddenly, she turned towards the target. With a gun in each hand she lifted them theatrically and pulled both triggers at the same time. Nothing happened. She laughed at their puzzled faces and returned the guns. "You try again."

One after the other, John and Brett both discharged their guns successfully. Gleefully, Diana asked them to swap guns and try again. Neither would fire. "Smart, eh?" she bubbled.

"What's going on?" John mumbled, distinctly less enthusiastic.

"These guns are like faithful dogs," she began. "They recognize their owners and won't perform for anyone else. There's a hidden sensor in the handle. It monitors your grip. The first time you fired, I programmed them to record your normal hand pressure, palm print and fingerprint. From that moment, they'll only perform when the chip senses the same grip. If someone else tries to fire it, no chance."

"That *is* smart," Brett observed.

"Yes," she said. "We call it the smart gun. You see, firearms technology has remained unchanged for ages. We weren't doing much better than Billy the Kid. This technology takes us into the next century. Every year in the States, hundreds of kids shoot themselves by accident when they get their hands on their parents' Smith & Wessons. And one in four American cops who get killed are shot with their own guns – when prisoners snatch their weapons. The smart gun will put a stop to all that. Surely even you'll approve, John."

"Mmm. If we *have* to be armed sometimes, I guess

it'll make the world a bit safer."

"OK," Diana chirped. "Time for you to retreat to separate booths. One hour's practice and time for me to make minor adjustments till you're happy with your individualized guns. When we're finished I'll store them here for you until you next need to be issued with firearms. The pair of you are lucky enough to be chosen to test the smart gun in the field."

Alone with the predatory Firearms Technician, Brett tried to keep his distance, and keep her mind on business. He'd decided that he could use her to test out a theory. Whispering so that John in the next booth could not hear, Brett enquired, "Are any of the senior officers still authorized to carry firearms? I guess several *were* licensed but do they keep it up? Do they come in for compulsory practice?"

"Not many," Diana replied. "You don't need to fire guns to do paperwork at a desk all day."

"But some do," Brett gathered. "What about Keith Johnstone, for example?"

"Yes, well, he's one of the few. I don't know why. Just likes to keep his hand in, I suppose. Or maybe he fancies me." She smiled vainly at the notion. "Anyway, he does come in regularly for his refreshers but he's not that good these days."

"Interesting," Brett muttered. So, Keith Johnstone still used guns, he thought. That was enough. No one has to be an expert marksman to shoot a victim at point-blank range. "Does *he* have a smart gun?"

"No. He's got a conventional thirty-eight," Diana answered. "You're the trail-blazer. So, you'd better crack on with your practice. I can't let you out of here until you've given me a convincing performance," she said, winking at him. "You need my signature on a report, confirming that you're up to scratch." She put her hand on his shoulder and added, "I could claim that you need some extra out-of-hours practice, if you like. I'd be happy to see you on your own. Private tuition."

Brett turned towards the target and pumped three bullets into its centre. "No," he said. "I don't think that's necessary. Besides, the Edale case is a round-the-clock job."

When she left him to it, he breathed a sigh of relief.

The fungus was growing on a bed of nutrients in a small glass bottle. A gentle flow of nitrogen gas blew the tiny amounts of chemicals from the fungus along a narrow plastic tube and into a trapping device. When enough of the chemicals had been collected, the trap was suddenly heated to release them all into the gas chromatograph. The grey box separated each substance and in turn swept them into the next device. The mass spectrometer completed the task of detecting and identifying all of the chemicals in the stream of gas.

Derek sat at the controlling computer of the GC/MS and Brett stood behind him, watching the results unfold on the monitor. "Active fungus, isn't it?" the professor commented. "Lots of peaks." Every time that a chemical was detected, a line leapt up from the bottom of the screen, formed a peak and, after a few seconds, returned to the bottom.

"Yes. A complex mixture," Brett noted. "Let's just concentrate on the major components."

"OK. It's your show," Derek replied. "I'll work on the five biggest peaks." He set the cursor on the first of the large peaks. When he tapped another key, a spectrum appeared. "It's a small sulphur compound," Derek deduced. "Disgustingly smelly." A few seconds later the computer reported that the substance causing the peak was dimethyl disulphide.

Derek examined the next peaks in the same way and concluded, "What you've got here is a pretty evil brew. Dimethyl trisulphide, ocimene, phenylacetaldehyde and phenylethanol."

"A natural product, an aldehyde and an alcohol," Brett murmured, recalling his library work. The same sort of chemicals that encouraged flies to lay their eggs. "Interesting." He asked Derek, "If our human noses were sensitive enough, what would that smell like?"

"Horrible. Ocimene's your only whiff of something pleasant — the smell of basil. Otherwise, it's utterly revolting. Like rotting flesh."

"And what would a fly make of it?"

Derek grinned. "Yummy! Rotting flesh — an incubator, lodgings and a canteen all in one handy package."

Brett laughed and nodded. "Good. I thought you might say that. Can I have a printout of these results?"

"Sure," the chemist said. "But are you going to tell me? *Have* I solved the crime of the century?"

"Not exactly," Brett replied. "But you've been a huge help. You've confirmed my suspicions that we've been barking up the wrong tree."

"Well," Derek said as he rose, "that's a pint you owe me – and one for the research student who got it all ready for us. Drop in again if I can help, but next time, see if there's a budget you can scrounge from. I need every penny I can get."

Brett thanked his old tutor and said, "I'll see what I can do. Anyway, you were right. It *was* nice to come back. Good to work with you again."

"You know, Brett, you should think about it in the future. You had a knack for this business. OK, you'd often come up with a brilliant, complicated idea to explain something and completely overlook the obvious simple answer, but there are much worse faults. You'd be welcome back."

Brett shook his tutor's hand warmly. "Thanks, but I think I'll take the results and run."

Derek chuckled. "I thought that's what you'd say. Oh, well. I tried."

Brett felt so pleased with himself and his discovery that on the way home he called at a supermarket to buy the ingredients for his favourite meal. Onions, green pepper, mushrooms and cheese. Tonight he was determined to indulge himself. He wasn't a vegetarian but he loved the flavour of a good mushroom roast. Besides, his body needed a break from animal fat. He went to bed feeling nourished and vindicated. Tomorrow, he would correct the time of death of Victim Number Four, and as a result, strengthen the case for looking into the most unlikely suspect, Detective Chief Superintendent Keith Johnstone, and his mystery Edale companion.

The morning air was muggy. A substantial haze tarnished the parkland. Brett ran through it, breathing evenly. In two hours, he estimated, a fierce sun would burn away the mist and leave a sweltering day. He was pleased to complete his run before he was scorched and dehydrated.

In the incident room, Big John announced that Brett had some new evidence and stood aside so that Brett could brief the team. "OK," he proclaimed. "The problem's Victim Number Four. I think he should really be Victim Number Two." There was a dissatisfied rumble among the ranks. They realized immediately that if Brett was correct, they had been tramping the country lanes asking the wrong questions about the dead teenager. He continued, "You know that pathology wanted an old time of death – up to six months ago – because of the decay of the body. Forensic entomology disagreed. The insect evidence seemed absolutely clear. The body was less than two weeks old. I now believe that's wrong and pathology got it right."

He explained, "Flies are attracted to odour trails of fresh bodies, but only for a few days after death. As soon as bodies are older than a few days, flies turn their noses up at them. Don't want to know. When the foxes brought Victim Number Four into the open air, flies deposited their eggs on him. When we got there, he was pretty lively with maggots so the entomologist decided it must have been a fresh body. Just a few days since death. It seemed logical. But, while he was buried, a fungus grew on him. That was the white powder. I had it analysed. When it meets the air, it gives off a stench that mimics rotting flesh. The local flies were confused by the chemical cocktail from the fungus. They thought it was a fresh dead body and made a bee-line for it. That's why they went into egg-laying mode – because of the fungus. Victim Number Four is weeks, maybe months, old."

"Back to the drawing board," someone moaned. The rest issued a communal groan.

Mark whispered to Greg, "Maybe not as superfluous as you thought."

Greg merely grimaced in reply.

"That's pretty good work, Brett," John congratulated him. "Means we've got to flood the area again.

This time, we ask if they've seen Victim Number Four in the past six months – not in the past couple of weeks."

John's pronouncement struck a chord with Brett. In Upper Needless, the man in the grocery shop, Zoe and Thomas had all been eager to deny seeing Victim Number Four in the past fortnight. Brett was keen to return to the village himself to see their reaction to a wider time frame. He would be particularly keen to interview Zoe, but he had more than one motive for wanting to talk to her again.

"And," John added, glancing at Brett, "now that the most recent victims include the baby, we ask about a missing child. You know the sort of thing. Did neighbours hear a baby crying and suddenly it stopped? OK. Let's get stuck in. Brett, I think you'll want to see me first."

Brett smiled wryly and nodded.

In his office, John prompted, "All right. Tell me again who you want investigated."

"You know," Brett said. "It's very important now to look at anyone who was in the area in May last year, Easter this year, and at the turn of the year – six months ago. We found only one person who fits that profile. Don't get me wrong. I'm not accusing him of anything, but we ought to eliminate him."

Big John flopped on to a seat and sighed wearily. His attitude towards Brett had changed. Suddenly, he had softened. "Yes. I have a suggestion, though. You crack on with organizing the Edale interviews.

Leave Keith Johnstone to me. It's delicate, to say the least."

"Is that wise?" Brett questioned. "You're rather close to him. A friend. You don't really regard him as a suspect."

"Don't push your luck, lad," John snapped. "Up to a point, you're right. I trust my senior colleague. Serial killers don't get to his rank. But because I know him well, I'm probably the only one who can talk to him about it without being sacked. That's all I can do."

Realizing that John was protecting him, Brett agreed. "OK. I'll leave it in your hands. But remember, he's not the only one. He could've taken someone with him."

Brett arranged the team for its next foray into the Vale of Edale. "I'll cover Upper Needless again," he said, "but this time I want to take Clare with me. I need to interview a woman who seems a bit sensitive: Zoe. Perhaps a female presence will help. OK with you, Greg?"

Greg shrugged churlishly. "You're the boss." The fact that Brett's opinion about Victim Number Four had been justified did not cut much ice with Greg.

"Did you find out any background on the village?"

"A crime-free zone," Greg answered. "Not even a meagre driving offence. They've probably never been fined for an overdue library book."

Once more, several cars were despatched to Edale. In one of them, Brett declared, "Gorgeous day. Nice not to be cooped up in the office in this weather."

"Maybe for you," Clare retorted. "Haven't you heard about redheads? Fair skin and freckles. Burn easily. A risk of skin cancer that's ten times the average white person's. It's like carrying your own personal ozone hole around with you. Anyway," she said, "I've come prepared." She extracted a small tube of sunscreen from her pocket. "Factor 25." She dabbed the cream liberally on her forehead, cheeks, nose and neck until she looked like a clown. Then she rubbed it in and muttered, "As good as a black plastic bag over my head."

"But a bit more attractive," Brett replied. "That's the appliance of science for you."

"That's right," Clare said. "You're into science, aren't you?"

"I've got a degree in biochemistry. Some of our colleagues think it's as useful and appealing as a dose of leprosy."

"You exaggerate. You're not the first graduate entrant who's had to work at it. This morning's briefing could help. You've proved it's useful. Now," she said with a cheeky expression, "you've got to work on the appeal."

"You're the one who referred to the squad as the testosterone club," he said. "What was that about?"

"Well, it sometimes feels like that. A macho club for men. Like any woman police officer, I had to work at it to get accepted. It took time. It'll be the same for you. Different reason, though."

"Yeah. My oestrogen levels are low enough," Brett joked, "but my qualifications are too high."

"Take my advice," Clare replied. "Forget it and get on with the job. Believe me, you'll only win them over by being good. Then, your IQ or gender won't matter. Think about Liz. She had two handicaps. Black *and* female. She had it rough. Whispers and whinges behind her back. Even the odd malicious note left on her desk. Horrible. But she persisted. Proved she's got what it takes. She's one of the lads now."

"Pity, in a way," Brett replied. "I wish she'd managed to change the lads rather than fit in with them."

Clare nodded slowly. "True. But if you can't beat 'em, join 'em, I suppose."

"I guess that's why you and Liz have been more tolerant towards me," Brett ventured. "You've been through it yourselves."

"Maybe," she said. Then she chuckled and added, "Greg and some of the others would say it's just our mothering instinct coming out."

"I never knew there were so many hormones loose in the police force," Brett responded with a smile on his face.

More serious, Clare said, "In a squad there's real friendship, the pursuit of a common goal, bonding, shared misery *and* shared triumphs. Powerful ties. Powerful emotions. With that sort of recipe, there's always jealousies, competition, hidden – and not so hidden – clashes as well. That's the other side of the same coin. You've got to take one with the other."

"I suppose so," Brett said. "A perfect world it ain't."

He liked Clare. She did not seem concerned with his superior rank. She offered advice, encouragement and criticism as a friend. That's what Brett expected of a true partnership.

"Police work must be quite a culture shock for you," she said. "Science deals with certainty. It's either right or wrong. There's no doubt."

"No," Brett answered. "People always seem to think that, but there's no absolute truth in science, you know. Someone has a theory and everyone else tries to knock it down. That's how it's done. Scientists don't prove things to be true, they just prove that bad theories are wrong. If they can't prove a theory wrong, then it's regarded as their best stab at the truth. There's no real certainty. If there was only one theory about something and everyone believed in it, you'd have religion, not science." He paused before adding, "A scientific investigation isn't so different from a police investigation. We prove a lot of people are innocent and what remains is the guilty. It's just that, for us, there's an extra step that science can't take. Proving the truth of that guilt."

"Ever thought of taking up lecturing?" Clare asked. Then she laughed.

"You don't have to put up with me much longer," Brett replied with a grin. "We're nearly there." He briefed her on what he knew of the village and Zoe Adamson.

To the sound of a barking dog, Brett parked the car by the farm and stepped into the medieval atmosphere of Upper Needless. He pulled up his shirt sleeves as if he were about to begin some manual work. Really, he just wanted to feel the warmth of the sun on his muscular arms. Clare joined him, the sleeves of her sweatshirt protecting her delicate skin from the sun. Brett had learned enough about her to know that her character and physique were more robust. She was confident, sleek and powerful. He guessed that she worked out regularly in a gym. As his partner, she transmitted some of her confidence to him.

Surveying the hamlet, she murmured, "It's quaint. Like one of those living museums."

The farmhouse was big and old. Two huge chimneys, recently repointed, clung to its sides. They looked as if they had been constructed as an afterthought and out of proportion with the rest of the building. In the farmyard, there was a wooden shed. From hooks on its wall, archaic tools were hanging like relics. A couple of rakes, some scythes, an enormous saw and several pitchforks. They should have been rusting and obsolete but instead they were smeared liberally with grease to keep them in good working order.

As Brett and Clare walked down the lane towards the village hall, the young children of the school were playing happily in the neighbouring field. It must have been morning break. Watching over the pupils, Zoe was standing in the school porch. Brett saw her and came to an abrupt halt. In the moment before she noticed him, she looked natural and serene. Against the dark seasoned brickwork, her slender form was exquisite. In an instant, the moment was spoiled. Clare stopped and asked, "What's up?" Then she saw Zoe and muttered perceptively, "Now I know why you wanted to take on this job yourself."

At the same time, Zoe spotted the police officers. Immediately, she peered up and down the road as if she was scared to be seen in their vicinity. When she realized that the lane was empty, she smiled at Brett as she walked cautiously towards him.

"Hello again," Brett said brightly.

Zoe nodded briefly towards him, brushed her hair behind her shoulders and murmured, "Back again, Detective Inspector Lawless?" Her voice was deep and seductive, with a noticeable accent that was not quite Derbyshire in origin. Perhaps the folk of Upper Needless were so isolated that they had developed a peculiar dialect of their own. "Do you want to speak to my uncle?"

"Not really," Brett answered. "We're more interested in speaking to you." He was pleased to be able to interview her without her uncle's intervention. He was also impressed that she had remembered his name and rank. Bringing Clare into play, he said, "This is Detective Sergeant Tilley.

We're sorry to bother you again but we need to make absolutely sure about this boy." Brett produced the likeness of the inappropriately named Victim Number Four. "Take another look and think if you've seen him in the past few months. Could be as much as six months ago."

"That's not what you said last time," Zoe commented.

"No," Clare interjected. "Since then we've come across new evidence. That's why we have to ask you again. Last time, you were trying to put his face in a recent context. Now you need to cast your mind back. What do you think? Can you remember someone like that?"

Brett watched Zoe's face. He was supposed to be deciphering her expressions and body language but he was simply mesmerized by her unassuming charm.

When she answered Clare's question, she addressed Brett. "I'm not so sure. I don't think so, but…"

"It's hard, I know," Clare said supportively, "but try to think of a setting where you might have seen him."

Her face began to show signs of distress. "Sorry," she replied. "I can't be sure. It's horrible. When I look at this picture, all I can think of is his death."

"That's all right," Brett replied. "Let's try something else." He glanced at Clare.

Clare continued the questioning. "Do you know anyone, a young woman, who had a baby about three months ago and who disappeared — along with the baby — almost straightaway?"

Zoe looked ruffled. Again talking to Brett, she replied, "That's even worse. I can't bear to think about it. Shooting a baby."

Brett put in, "This woman suffered a cut to her shin once." He bent down and touched his left leg just above the ankle. "About here," he said. "Does that help?"

Behind Zoe, a bell sounded. She looked like a bruised boxer at the end of a round: shaken but relieved. "Sorry. I've got to go," she said. "I'm helping out in the school today." The children had formed a line and were filing back inside. "All right?"

Brett glanced at Clare and together they nodded. "Thanks anyway," Brett said.

Looking over her shoulder, she replied, "Sorry I'm not much help. Bye."

They both watched till she dashed inside, then Clare sighed.

"Well, what do you think?" asked Brett.

"She's not telling us everything but there was no point prolonging it here and now. She's not going to open up here in the street." Clare paused before she added, "If you don't mind criticism, I think you got your tactics all wrong. If you want to find out what she really knows, you don't want me with you. You don't want *anyone* with you. I reckon she's got a soft spot for you. She hardly looked at me. It was all you. Truth be told, she seemed to resent the fact that you had a woman with you. I was treading on her patch. If you want to exploit her weakness, you should do it on your own. In private. Preferably away from this place. That's the way to get her to talk."

"Ever thought of taking up lecturing?" Brett teased her. "Seriously, though," he added, "you might be right."

"You need another excuse to come back again."

"I've already got that," Brett remarked. "In the farm there was a flock of sheep. I noticed that three of them had a red splodge on their right flanks. That identifies them as George Bottomley's animals. He's the farmer near the wood where the bodies were found. And he's been complaining about sheep rustling."

"Stolen sheep! Derbyshire Constabulary should handle that. It's what they're good at – sheep rustling," she said with a grin. "Haven't we got enough on our hands without you playing Wild West sheriff?"

"I'm not. If an angry Bottomley caught some youngsters from here pinching his sheep, who knows what he might do to them."

"So why wouldn't Zoe just tell us that her mates hadn't come back from their sheep raid? Don't tell me you think she's too ashamed of their stealing sheep to admit it!"

Brett shrugged. "I don't know. I keep an open mind. And before you ask, I don't know why a new mother and her baby would go on a raid, either."

Together, they strolled through the village, knocking on doors and enquiring about Victim Number Four and the baby. Whenever she could, Clare positioned herself in the shade, out of the harsh sunshine. The responses at each doorstep cast no further light on their investigation. They learned only that their inquiry was not welcome in Upper Needless.

On the way back to Sheffield, Brett proposed that they should stop for a meal and get to know one another. He anticipated that he'd stand a better chance of consuming a nutritious dinner with Clare than with John.

"OK," she agreed. "I know a great place in Hathersage. A fish restaurant that serves superb real ale."

"Fish?" Brett queried with a frown on his face.

"You don't eat fish, I take it," Clare surmised. "What happened? Food poisoning after fish and chips when you were a toddler?"

"No," Brett replied, "I like fish, that's all. Swimming, as opposed to lying on a plate."

Instead, they called at an Indian restaurant and talked about each other. Brett learnt that his favourite colleague was twenty-five years old and had joined the police force direct from school. She was single, had a weakness for good beer, kept in trim with several styles of karate, and hated knives when used as weapons. She had joined the police because she wanted to make the world a safer, happier place.

In uniform, she had done a lot of work with young offenders until her ability to deal effectively with people took her to the CID under Big John's wing. She hadn't looked back. She relished the big cases, possessed infinite patience, enjoyed the team work, and loved barbecued red snapper. She admired music but disliked fashion. Instead of becoming more cynical and suspicious by being a police officer, she had become more sympathetic and understanding of people's problems. She was content in a job that could still make her laugh or cry. She read poetry, hated opera, and closed her eyes in the scary bits of horror films. She illustrated beautifully that the guardians of law and order were not heroes and heroines but ordinary mortals who cared.

"You know," she said, "no one would call Zoe a social animal. I bet her circle of friends is limited. If she's hiding something about the victims – if she knows them – the chances are they're from Upper Needless."

"Yes," Brett agreed. "Or there is another possibility. I've seen for myself there's a good deal of animosity between the Upper Needless folk and the rest of the locals. Some of them, anyway. Perhaps the victims were youngsters from Hope or wherever who went to the village to make trouble and the villagers took the law into their own hands. Now they're having to keep quiet about it, but the guilt's weighing heavy on Zoe. She's beginning to feel the pressure."

"I'm not convinced they'd take a baby with them.

And, remember, no one's been reported missing from round here. Besides, in a way, the victims were a bit like Zoe," Clare argued. "No fancy clothes. No jewellery. No dental work. I bet the people of Upper Needless don't bother much with dentists."

"No one's been reported missing from Upper Needless either. If the victims were from there, why isn't anyone saying so?" Answering his own question, Brett said, "Possibly for fear of reprisals. Perhaps they've been threatened with even worse if they talk." He hesitated and then continued, "If you're right, Clare – if they were from Upper Needless – I know a suspect. I even spoke to him. When I first drove out to the wood, a lad in Hope was virtually assaulting an old man in the street, on the grounds that his car had broken down and that he came from Upper Needless. It seemed to incense him. He'd fit John's profile of a serial killer. He could be on a mission to rid the world of 'undesirables' from Upper Needless."

"But you don't know who he was?"

"No. He was driving – let me think – a red Mondeo. He could have been from anywhere but I gathered he was local, maybe from Hope. When we get back, we'll get Mark and Liz to dig out Mondeo owners in the Hope, Castleton and Edale area," Brett decided. "But let's not forget, if the victims *were* outsiders who'd fallen foul of someone in Upper Needless, the killer would have stripped any identifying features from the bodies before dumping them. That could be why they resemble Upper Needless folk. The best evidence we've got for identification is the stuff that can't be erased. The boy with the strong left arm and the girl with a nick out of her shin bone. Anyway," Brett added, "let's pay the bill and get back. It's been good to talk to you."

"Yes, it has," Clare said with a mischievous grin. "You're not as bad as they're saying, Detective Inspector."

Brett smiled wryly. "Thanks for the vote of confidence."

"Unfortunate. I think that was the word you used last time," John said across the giant desk.

"Most likely," Keith replied. "Do I take it that you have further unfortunate coincidences to report?"

"Thanks to some diligent work by your new boy, we now have a different time of death for one of our victims. He's not a few days old but possibly months old. Six months has been suggested. New Year."

"New Year. So, my wife and I have been in the area whenever a murder has occurred. No wonder you wanted to see me again. Are you telling me to get a good lawyer?" The playful glint in his eye did not quite match his stern expression.

"How long have I known you, Keith? Since the dinosaurs ruled. I know you too well to hold the remotest suspicion. But just think how it looks to Brett and a few of the others on the team. They don't really know you. They just see the evidence."

"What are you saying, John?"

"Two things, I guess. I'm saying when you were younger, you would have seized on a lead like this. Don't come down on Brett too heavily if he does what comes naturally to a copper. And couldn't you give me an account of your weekends that puts you out of the picture? That way, Brett can drop the idea altogether."

"When Rebecca and I go to the Peaks, we walk, we take in the air. She goes off to her beloved country stores and I read or have a drink or two." The Chief shrugged. "I'm not going to lie simply to provide you with a convenient alibi. What you have to get Lawless to appreciate is that our whole operation depends on trust – especially in whoever happens to be sitting in this chair. If there isn't confidence in the Chief, the whole system starts to fall apart. I don't want to hear the faintest creak. I leave the matter in your hands, John. I want to get on with my job and I don't want Rebecca upset either. Now," he said, changing the subject, "you seem to be a bit happier with Brett Lawless."

Big John smiled. "I guess so. He's been useful, at least in this case. He discovered something no one else would have picked up. But it won't be that way in every case. Give him the right inquiry and he'll do a job all right, I suppose. I'm still not sure why he's in the police force, though. Forensic science is more his cup of tea. I haven't seen enough of him yet, but from what I have seen, I'd say he's no great judge of character. A halfway decent actor would fool him every time. Still, he has his strengths. If we do keep him, he needs the right partner. Someone like me – but not me. Brett would take care of the logic and reasoning all right, but the partner would have to be good at understanding people. In the right team, he could be an asset."

Keith Johnstone grinned. "Coming from you, that's high praise!"

"Yeah, well, he was right and I was wrong on a major issue so I can't be too critical."

"Keep me informed – of *all* developments," Keith ordered. "And, believe me, I do understand Brett's problem with this circumstantial evidence, but we can't let morale and discipline slip, John."

On the seventh day of the investigation, Brett was supposed to get a rest. But he knew that if he tried to take a day off, it would last until his pager reminded him that the only realistic time for a holiday was between one case and the next. Instead of a break, he took a longer jog than normal in the morning. It was not the stuff of marathon runners but he felt pleasantly tested afterwards. It seemed opportune, on a day that he was not supposed to be on duty, to make a solo visit to Upper Needless.

As he drove on familiar roads to the Vale of Edale, he radioed his intentions to headquarters. On Burbage Moor, hikers followed well-worn tracks across the wild, treeless plateau. Writhing alarmingly, the road plummeted into Hathersage, shaded from the bright morning sun by the dominating hill behind. Down in the valley, the lush fields were divided neatly by dry-stone walls, making a monochrome chessboard in green. A line of trees would separate one property from another. Some of the trees were dead, forming tortured shapes, yet they remained tenaciously upright. The slopes that formed the sides of the valley were kept in the shade by their own bare ridges. The pattern of dark patches was completed by the shifting shadows of the occasional clouds. It was a warm, agreeable day – far too nice to probe callous murders. But Brett was spurred by impatience, a desire to find an answer. Mysteries annoyed him.

In Upper Needless, the farm was maintained by a number of the villagers. It was like a commune, run for the benefit of the whole village. The man who lived in the farmhouse and who appeared to be in charge was Ryan Kemp. Brett found him in the farmyard, mending implements and sharpening cutting tools. He was about fifty and the hairiest person Brett had ever seen. Thick curls of hair dangled down to his brow and his ample beard started high on his cheeks. His eyes seemed to stare out from a nest and his ears were hidden entirely. The small area of visible skin was wrinkled, dark and leathery.

Forgetting his senior officer's advice about handling farmers, Brett plunged straight in. "Your sheep," he began. "They're unmarked."

"Yes," Ryan stated bluntly as if expecting a verbal onslaught.

"Except for a few that are marked with a red dye."

"What do you mean?" the farmer asked.

"Do you know George Bottomley?"

"No."

"So," Brett enquired, "why have you got some of his sheep?"

"I thought you was investigating a murder," Ryan said.

"I am. I'm also looking into some missing sheep. Now," Brett asked again, "can you explain why some of Bottomley's sheep are among your flock?"

"Simple," Ryan muttered, looking up into Brett's face. "We run a good farm here. It's a good, traditional life. Good for us. Good for the livestock. It wouldn't surprise me if a few sheep joined us."

Incredulous, Brett hesitated but was unable to keep a straight face. He chuckled before responding, "Mr Kemp, I'm no expert on the psychology of sheep but I find it hard to believe that they'd come to a rational decision to change their lifestyles and set out of their own accord to find this particular Utopia. Besides, we're about a mile away from the Bottomley farm and there's a road and a railway between there and here. I think that's asking a lot of the sheep. Don't you?"

"Sheep range far and wide round these parts," Ryan claimed.

"Even so..."

"Maybe they were chased away from home territory by a tourist's dog. It happens, you know. Regular. Maybe they ended up here."

"Are you sure it wasn't you and your own sheep-dog that brought them here on purpose?"

"No. I didn't do that."

"Well, has anyone in the village – any of your helpers – been to Bottomley's farm to poach his sheep?"

"Not so's I know. We don't wander much – not like the sheep."

Brett recognized that he wasn't going to extract any more from Ryan Kemp so he changed tack. "Does Zoe ever help out on the farm?"

Ryan's face creased. "The Adamson girl? Yes. Just about everyone does sometimes."

"Is she here now?"

Ryan shook his head.

"Where will I find her?"

"School," Ryan replied. "It's her turn to help there this week." He looked up at the sky, and following his gaze, Brett realized that he was estimating the time by the sun's position. "Soon be their break."

"Thanks," Brett said. He turned to go.

"What are you going to do about the sheep?" Ryan called after him. Nonchalantly, as if he weren't really interested in the answer, Ryan picked up a blunt scythe, ready to sharpen its long curved blade.

"I'm busy on a serious investigation at the moment," Brett pronounced. "If George Bottomley's sheep accidentally wandered back to their rightful owner – or if a farmer and his collie drove them back

– I doubt if I'd remember to report the incident once the murder case is wrapped up."

Brett waited outside the primary school, hoping that Zoe would appear again. When the small group of children spilled out into the play area, she accompanied them. She squatted down to talk to three boys who were arguing heatedly. When she had calmed them down she stood up, noticed Brett and flushed. Stopping to help a girl who seemed to have lost something, she met Brett at the gate.

"Back again?" she enquired.

"Yes. But I'm not on business," Brett told her. "It's social." Nervously, he asked, "Can you take a bit of time off? I wondered if you wanted to come for a stroll. You could show me the valley, perhaps. Then we could have lunch maybe?"

For a moment, Zoe looked reticent and shocked. But she also looked pleased. She murmured, "I don't know." She was keen to accept the invitation from an off-duty Brett, but she was wary of Brett the police officer. "It *would* be nice but…" She peered into his face briefly, remembered his heroics in Hope, and made up her mind to trust him. "Just a minute." She went back into the school, and after a couple of minutes, emerged again. "Yes," she breathed. "The teacher doesn't need me till after lunch. But," she added, glancing around, "can we go somewhere else?" Obviously, she wanted to get away from the prying eyes of the village. "If we go down the lane in your car, there's a place we can stop and get on to the uplands. I can show you some nice sights."

"Sounds good to me," Brett replied happily. He was surprised and delighted that she needed little persuasion to go with him. And he felt guilty that he was about to betray her trust. He valued her friendship but he also valued the information that he believed she was concealing.

"Wow!" she exclaimed as she got into Brett's car and he started it. "I've never been in a car like this. It's not like Grandfather's old thing. So quiet and smooth. And all the equipment!"

Brett smiled at her childlike glee. "Nothing really special about it – apart from the radio," he explained.

Later, after they had clambered up Horsehill Tor, they had the same conversation in reverse. Brett stared at an outcrop of millstone grit and marvelled at the shapes. The layered stacks of rock looked like the profiles of three faces. An angry old man with a huge nose. A flat-headed and startled tortoise with an elongated cavity for a mouth, a round hole for an eye and a thick, wrinkly neck. A smiling woman with a fat dimpled cheek and prominent brow. "Great shapes! I've never seen anything like that."

"My favourite rocks. They've been here for three hundred million years, you know."

"Three hundred million years, eh? You don't look that old to me."

Zoe giggled. "That's what it says in books."

"They've seen a lot of life – and death," Brett

commented.

Thoughtfully, Zoe muttered, "I suppose so."

Brett and Zoe turned round and surveyed the vale. They were almost in line with the railway that punctured the hill beneath them. To the left, some of the buildings of Upper Needless were visible, made tiny by distance. The pure expanse of nature took Brett's breath away. Zoe seemed pleased that one of her haunts could enchant him. There were no paths. They were some distance from the popular Pennine Way. Yet Zoe was on home territory. She picked out tracks made by the sheep and guided Brett to the best views and strangest rock formations. Selecting a couple of flat rocks, they sat for a while and savoured the scenery and fresh air.

"That first time, in Hope last week," Zoe said, "you never said you were a policeman."

"It wasn't necessary," Brett ventured. "And I'm not a traffic cop, anyway."

"Yes, but that lad was going to hurt us. I've been brought up to believe that outsiders don't care about me – let alone come to my rescue."

Brett replied with sincerity, "That's sad. Not everyone's so indifferent, you know. Anyway," he added, "*you* didn't say anything at all."

"That wasn't necessary either. But I would've done. Because you were different – and kind," she added coyly. "I wanted to say thanks but Grandfather wouldn't have approved of speaking to strangers."

Two sure-footed sheep wandering over the uplands

halted, looked at them suspiciously, then hurried away timidly.

"Do these sheep ever go down to your farm?" Brett queried.

"Yes. Usually in winter when it gets pretty inhospitable up here. When they get hungry."

"Do they wander very far? Would you get some from farms over there?" He waved his hands towards Bottomley's farm below them on the right.

Zoe frowned at his sudden curiosity.

"Sorry," Brett said. "It's hard not to talk shop a bit. But it's all off the record."

Her hair stirred in the breeze and she pulled some strands away from her face. "I won't get anyone into trouble?"

"Promise," Brett replied. "I'm not in the sheep squad," he added with a smile.

"Well, some of the boys sneak on to other farms. Not often – just when the flock gets a bit low. They take the dog and come back with a couple of extra sheep."

Brett sighed. "Risky," he remarked. "What happens if they get caught?"

Zoe shrugged. "They're careful."

"Have any of them got into trouble with local farmers?"

She hesitated and then answered, "No."

"They've always come back in one piece?"

"Of course."

"And do any girls go on these raids?"

"I don't think so. I haven't," she said.

"What *do* you do?" Brett enquired. "Help out in the school. Do a bit on the farm. Anything else?"

"A bit of everything, really," she informed him. "We all muck in. We all have to pull our weight. Most of us follow a craft as well. Mine's sketching."

"Interesting. But how do you earn your money?"

"We don't need much. We sell produce at markets and to the tourists at craft fairs. That sort of thing. It keeps us going. And, many years ago, there was a man called Matthew Robinson who loved the area. He bought a cottage here for his retirement, and left a fortune to the village in his will. Uncle Thomas takes care of it. It's invested and the interest is ploughed into the village. There's an annual top-up as well. It all helps. Besides, there are more important things than wealth, you know."

Brett looked into her pretty face and said, "True." For a minute they appreciated the countryside in silence. Then Brett asked, "Don't you ever want to break out and – I don't know – see the world, sample city life?"

"How can you say that when you see this?" Zoe replied, indicating the landscape. "It's beautiful."

Brett noted that she hadn't really answered the question. He observed, "Sometimes, home looks even better when you've been away."

Zoe did not respond and Brett did not pursue it.

Brett looked at his watch and said, "What about a bite to eat? We could drive into Edale."

Zoe looked at him with the naïve and cheerful expression of someone who had never before been asked out for a meal. "OK," she murmured, turning away quickly in a vain attempt to hide her embarrassment and satisfaction.

She seemed to glide down the hillside towards the car while Brett, much more awkward, slipped and stumbled. He was slow and unsure at one moment of the descent and sliding virtually out of control at the next. During the drive to Edale, Brett's radio crackled into life. It was Mark. "You gave us a tough time with this red Mondeo," he reported. "The boys and girls in blue have been chasing round all morning, narrowing it down to young drivers. The most likely-looking candidate is one Glenn Troke. His father came up on the database as the owner of a red Mondeo. Lives in Castleton. The local cops say they know Glenn Troke. Nineteen-year-old who passed his test a few months ago. As you're out there, I thought you might want to drop in on him." He read out the Trokes' address.

"Why do they know him?" Brett queried. "What's he been up to?"

"Vandalism, breaking and entering. That sort of thing. Nothing particularly malicious."

"OK. Thanks," Brett replied. "Good work. I'll see him on the way back." Really, Brett wanted to ask Mark to work on another lead that Zoe had inadvertently given him. But, with Zoe in the car, he could not admit to profiting from talking to her.

"So much for not being on duty," Zoe muttered disappointedly.

"I'm not," Brett said in his defence, but not entirely truthfully. "It's my day off. Because they knew I was out here, they couldn't resist getting me to do a bit of moonlighting. Saving resources. That's all. I assure you," he added with sincerity, "I'm here because I wanted to see you."

Zoe flushed and smiled to herself.

Over a chunky ploughman's lunch in the rugged pub, Brett decided to push his luck. "Let me be honest, Zoe," he began in a hushed voice. "These murders I'm working on. Yesterday – when it was official – we thought you might know more than you were saying. Now, when it's off the record and you're away from Upper Needless, I wondered if you wanted to tell me any more. Anything you say wouldn't get back to the village, if you've been told to keep quiet. I promise."

Zoe's head drooped. She stared at her food rather than at Brett and fiddled nervously with a crusty piece of bread. "Is this why you asked me out?" she mumbled.

"No," he replied firmly. "I asked you out because you're you. I enjoyed the walk, the views. I'm enjoying the meal with you. Really. And I enjoy seeing men walk in, hardly able to keep their eyes off you," he blurted out.

"That's because I'm a curiosity – from Upper Needless."

"Maybe. But not many know that." He felt flattered to be with her yet he did not say so because he didn't want to overstep the mark. "When this investigation's finished and I don't have any more business in Edale," Brett added, "I hope you'll still invite me to your favourite places." When she looked at him across the table and searched his face, he said, "Perhaps then you'll be convinced, but right now, I do have a case on my hands and I need you to tell me anything you know. I need to know the identities of those murdered youngsters." Impassioned, he uttered, "If they were alive today they'd be younger than you, Zoe. They were just kids."

Her eyes moist, Zoe sighed and put down the bread. Taken aback by Brett's ardour, she replied, "I know. It's awful. But…"

"Yes?"

She looked up at the pub's clock and muttered, "I should be getting back to the school. Besides, I can't talk in here. Will you meet me tomorrow?"

"Yes," Brett responded eagerly. "Where?"

"At the stones. The tortoise head. After school. Four o'clock."

"Do you want me to bring Sergeant Tilley with me?"

Zoe considered it for a moment, then answered, "No. Not really. I'd prefer it if it was just you."

"I'll be there – on my own," Brett promised, standing up.

They left the pub and drove the three miles back

to Upper Needless in almost complete silence. Zoe looked as gorgeous as ever but inside she seemed wretched, as if some forbidden knowledge was eating her away. Before she got out of the car in the village, she muttered, "Thanks for the lunch." She paused before adding, "Just be careful this afternoon if that lad you're going to see is a bit of a ruffian."

Brett smiled at her concern. "Don't worry. I can take care of myself."

Suddenly, Thomas appeared beside the car and tapped on Brett's window. As soon as Brett started to wind it down, the elder barked through the widening gap, "I really must protest at this continual harassment of my niece."

Calmly, Brett responded, "It's not harassment, I assure you. I'm off duty – just interested in the area. Zoe agreed to show me round the uplands. And very nice it is. That's all."

"Oh," Thomas snapped, still scowling. "Well, I'm glad you find us so attractive." Turning to Zoe, he said, "Time *you* were back inside. You know your help is needed." Plainly, he was annoyed with her. His tone was intimidating.

After she had entered the school, Thomas said to Brett, "I apologize if I seem rather protective. Since her father died, I have taken on that role. She's my brother's daughter, Inspector Lawless, but I regard her as my own."

Brett was puzzled as to why a woman of Zoe's age needed such supervision. At twenty years old, she was hardly a kid any more. Thomas Adamson had some sort of hold over her, Brett gathered. "That's understandable," he replied, "but we all need a little slack."

"Perhaps, Inspector, but we live a very sheltered life here. And so it will remain," he pronounced enigmatically as he walked away.

Brett shook his head and then shrugged. He put the car into reverse and spun round. "Next stop – Castleton," he muttered. Instead of driving back past Edale, he went the other way round the loop that connected Edale, Castleton and Hope. First, he took the narrow twisting road up the side of Mam Tor then, almost immediately, he turned left and descended between the enormous bleak, pale rocks of Winnats Pass. It was the most treacherous, spectacular and precipitous of the passes but not widely used since Mam Tor had shrugged the original wider road off its side like an unwelcome visitor. That scar had healed but Winnats Pass was still open. Its steep slope prohibited large vehicles and, in bad weather, it was the first pass to be closed. Whenever nature wished to exercise its power, it prevailed against the puny constructions of humankind.

Brett's car thundered across the cattle grid by Speedwell Cavern and headed along the valley to Castleton where the tourist shops were dominated by jewellery made from the stones of the Blue John Cavern. He pulled into the main car park and searched for the Trokes' house on foot.

12

A huge woman filled the doorway and mumbled, "What do you want?"

"I'm Detective Inspector Lawless," he announced, showing his identification. "And I'd like a word with Glenn."

"Well, he ain't in," the woman snarled.

At the back of the house, a door slammed shut and Brett guessed who had just left in a hurry. "Thank you very much," he retorted sarcastically. Scanning the row of houses, he spotted an entry further along the road. He made a dash for it. He sprinted between the houses and emerged on to a tarmac path beside a stream, separated from it by a bland stone wall. He saw a lad charging up the track, out of the small town. Brett groaned to himself and set off in pursuit. He loved to run but it lost all of its exhilaration when it became a chase. It was a corruption of a noble sport. For a big man, Brett was fast on his feet. At once, he began to narrow the gap but the young man had got a good start on him. Brett ran along the path and dashed over a bridge so that the brook was now on his left. Leaving behind the houses and the wall, the path began to rise towards Peak Cavern. Breathing harder, Brett closed on his tiring quarry. Now, the stream was in a deep grassy channel. The path continued to slope up. He watched as Glenn Troke, struggling hard, glanced over his shoulder, his face contorted with fatigue. Brett caught him up at the wide, shadowy mouth of the cavern. Trapped in front of the pay booth, the panting youth turned on Brett menacingly.

"Don't do anything silly, Glenn," Brett warned him. "As far as I know, you haven't done anything yet. So don't be rash. If you make a move on a police officer, you'll be in deep trouble. You know that. I don't want you to make things difficult for yourself."

Between gasps, Glenn said, "You're the cop who had a go at me last week in Hope. You've been following me about. That's police harassment."

Twice in the same day, Brett had been accused of harassment. He shook his head. "No. That's not true. I didn't have a go at you, and last week was a coincidence."

"Huh!" Glenn sneered.

"Why did you run?" Brett asked.

"Why do you think? Because there was a good

chance of getting away. I didn't know you were Linford Christie."

"But why try to get away?"

"I told you. Harassment," Glenn snorted. "Because police spells trouble. Always has. Always will. Always got it in for me."

"I haven't," Brett said in an amicable tone. He put out his hand to lay it in a conciliatory fashion on Glenn's shoulder, but the lad recoiled hastily. Instead, Brett tried to put him at ease by reasoning with him again. "I just want to talk to you about…"

Abruptly, Glenn set off, barging with his shoulder into Brett. It was like hitting an immovable rock. Glenn bounced off, lost his footing and tumbled down the bank into the stream. Brett winced as the lad's head cracked against a stone and he splashed, unconscious, into the stream. The clear water drifting past Glenn's head magically turned red. A sickening magic. Brett scrambled down the bank. Clinging with one hand to a thick exposed root and summoning all his strength, he dragged Glenn out of the water with the other. Then he clawed his way back up the steep embankment, hauling Glenn behind him as gently as he could. The young man was limp, a dead weight made worse by the water that had soaked into his clothes. Water trickled from both of his saturated trouser legs, like two over-flowing drainpipes.

As soon as he had pulled Glenn's body free of the gorge, Brett shouted into the ominously dark Peak

Cavern. The attendant's face peeped out of the gloom and Brett yelled to him, "Have you got a phone in there?"

The man nodded. "Yes. Is he hurt?"

"Call an ambulance. I'll meet it at the bottom of this path." Without hesitating, Brett picked up Glenn's unresponsive body and held him like a big baby. Bracing himself, he made his way back down the track to the main road, carrying the injured lad in his arms.

Once Glenn had been whisked away in an ambulance, Brett radioed headquarters to report the incident to John and then drove back. When he entered the incident room, voices bounced from one side to another like tennis balls. "Greg," Brett called. "Something for you. The good people of Upper Needless had a windfall some time ago. An inheritance from a Matthew Robinson. Some firm of solicitors round here must have handled the will. See if you can chase it down. They must still have records. The details could be interesting."

Greg grunted in response.

"Did you get anything out of Zoe Adamson?" Clare yelled across the room.

"Tomorrow afternoon. She knows something. She'll tell me then, I hope." Addressing the room at large, Brett asked, "Any success with the pictures?"

No one seemed to want to volunteer the information to Brett so Clare answered, "Possible sighting of the girl in Castleton. It's logged in the computer but it's too tenuous to be worthwhile. Nothing else."

"Nothing on the baby?"

"No."

"Good news from the hospital," Big John interjected. "Glenn Troke's conscious. We can talk to him."

"What's the bad?" someone queried, assuming that there was some.

"He's lodging a complaint against Detective Inspector Lawless. Claims his head wound was a result of being thumped by a brutal police officer. He says he didn't fall down a bank and hit his head on a stone."

Brett cursed under his breath.

"Don't worry about it,'" John said to Brett, "but you're off the interview, I'm afraid. I'll take Clare instead. We'll do the questioning and at the same time I'll see if his accusation's going to stick. Until I find out how damaging it is, you're still on the case. But keep away from him. Don't go near the hospital – and don't get into any more scrapes."

Brett sighed. His conscience was clear but he felt unsettled by the charge against him. Trying to put it to the back of his mind, he made a brief visit to the Chief Forensic Pathologist. He wanted to confirm a hunch that had occurred to him in Upper Needless. Finding Tony Rudd in the bare white morgue, meticulously measuring knife wounds on a male corpse, Brett interrupted, "Remember my Victim

Number Two? Any chance that the cut on her leg was caused by a scythe? She could have been using one to cut down weeds, crops or whatever. A careless swipe at the base of a plant could have caught her own leg low down and slightly on the upward swing. A pure accident. What do you think?"

Tony considered it but he did not stop his intricate analysis. "Possibly," he concluded. "The wound would be consistent with a scythe. But who uses them these days?"

Brett smiled. On his way out, he purred, "I know one place they're still used."

Deprived of extracting information from Glenn Troke, Brett went home early, collected his rugby gear and reported for training. After all, it was his day off. He tried hard to put his heart into the practice but whenever he crunched against a colleague, he thought of Glenn. He had the distinct impression that, when Glenn made a reckless bid for freedom, he was trying to escape arrest for some petty crime. If he were the serial killer, surely he would have pulled a gun on Brett. That was the murderer's style. That was his weapon of choice. Mark's research suggested that Glenn was more likely to wield a brick and threaten only window panes.

After working up a good sweat, Brett was informed by the coach that he had not shown enough commitment and concentration to be picked for the first team next season. Brett nodded regretfully, accepting the verdict. He had to acknowledge that, as his responsibilities grew, his free time would diminish. The criminal world would not declare a truce each time that Brett needed to attend a training session or a match.

On his way home, he picked up a curry. While he consumed it, he called the incident room and asked about Glenn Troke. A brain scan had revealed no permanent damage and he was recuperating. The interview with John and Clare had been halted by a concerned doctor. They aimed to see him in the morning instead. Brett had his own plans for a different interview in the morning. Zoe remained his best lead but he could not see her until the afternoon, so he had some time to investigate a loose end.

13

He had to be patient but eventually the hotel manageress granted him an audience. "Detective Inspector Lawless," she proclaimed with a puzzled expression as she walked into the spotless office where Brett was waiting. "What can I do for you?"

"I'm making some inquiries about –" He took a breath before adding, "Keith Johnstone. A client of yours." Brett knew that John had told him to avoid further snares, but his investigative mind had got the better of him. Besides, it was possible that the manageress could provide his chief with a secure alibi. With a few words, she could eliminate him cleanly from the inquiry. Hypothesis disproved.

The creases on the hotelier's face deepened. "You do know who he is, don't you?" Her tone implied that Brett was being indiscreet and unreasonable.

"Yes," Brett replied tersely.

"Detective Chief Superintendent Johnstone." She stated it as if his full title should strike fear into Brett's heart.

Brett persisted by asking, "When he stays here, he comes with – who?"

"His wife, Rebecca, of course," she answered protectively.

"And, typically, what does he do?"

"Do? He samples the country life. He goes out walking. He reads a lot in the lounge and bar."

"To your knowledge, does he go shooting at all?"

The manageress shrugged. "I'm not aware that he does. I rather suspect that he comes here to get away from that sort of thing."

"And his wife? Does she accompany him? Does she join him for walks and in the lounge?"

"Mrs Johnstone will walk with him sometimes but otherwise keeps her own schedule." She continued, "I understand that she enjoys shopping for Blue John trinkets and antiques."

"She goes off on her own, shopping?"

"I believe so."

"And she returns with souvenirs?"

"Inspector Lawless, I am not a police officer. I don't spy on my guests. In this hotel we enjoy respected and trustworthy clients. I count many of them as my friends." Her final sentence was meant as a distinct threat.

Brett smiled, thanked her for her co-operation and

151

left – without a solid alibi for his chief. He was not much wiser but, if Keith Johnstone was still a suspect because he'd always been in the vicinity when a murder had been committed, Rebecca Johnstone was equally tainted. And her movements in the Vale of Edale seemed to be more questionable than her husband's. Brett believed that his inquiries in Upper Needless were bringing him closer to the identities of the victims. He was less convinced that Zoe would also bring him closer to the murderer. He or she could be from anywhere. Until there was an arrest Brett had a duty to investigate the Johnstones, even if he had to tread a dangerous path. During his time at university, he had learned that scientists were driven by insatiable curiosity. As a detective, he was at the mercy of the same native compulsion. He needed to check out every possibility.

With the car door open, Brett sat sideways in the seat with his legs outside. By radio-telephone, he was listening to Big John's account of his interview with Glenn Troke. In his customary brief assessment of character, John dismissed the young man as a serious suspect. "He's a bit wayward, that's all. He's no serial killer. He's just panicked by us police. There's a real reason for his hostility towards the people of Upper Needless, though." Glenn had told John that, a year ago, his twenty-year-old brother Rob had been fooling around with a young woman from the village – Emma. Glenn did not know her surname. John gathered that Rob did not care about Emma at all. The whole thing was a big joke, a cruel joke, on the village. The Trokes seemed to believe that anyone with an offbeat lifestyle was fair game for ridicule. Emma was a particularly soft target for Rob's amusement. One evening, some men from Upper Needless had discovered Rob with Emma and given him a thorough beating. His cuts, bruises, broken nose and ribs had to be patched up in hospital. "Interesting, eh?"

"Very," answered Brett.

"Does the timing mean anything to you?" John enquired.

"Depends what you're getting at."

"I thought you were supposed to be good at biology and all that. A year ago would be the time that Victim Number Two got pregnant. She had a new-born baby three months ago." Unnecessarily, he teased, "Nine months plus three months equals one year."

"Yes. I took maths as well," Brett retorted. He was on edge because of his impending meeting with Zoe and because he was waiting impatiently for Big John to get around to discussing the charge of assault against him. "You're wondering if Victim Number Two is this Emma, and if Rob is the father of her baby. It's an interesting alternative to Greg's theory that Victim Number One was the father – on the same basis of timing. Where's our potential father now?"

"Ah," John said. "Another tasty fact. He left for a job in London two months ago."

"After the latest killing," Brett surmised. "He's a potential murderer as well, then."

"Yes," John stated. "He could have got his own back on a couple of the lads who beat him up. Then he could have taken his revenge on Emma, and the baby." He paused significantly and then added, "We really need your contact to come up trumps today, Brett. Don't mess it up." There was another hesitation before he continued, "And talking of messing up, Troke is definitely going to pursue his complaint against you. Insists you thumped him without good cause. He's lying, of course. I can tell. And I can tell you're not that sort of cop. I don't have a problem with your version of the events. It's just that Glenn Troke's decided to get his own back on the police force – through you. Like his brother tried to humiliate a whole village through one of its daughters. It must run in the family. Proving he's lying about you is a different matter, though. You keep out of it altogether. Don't do anything stupid to clear your name. You'll only dig a deeper hole for yourself. I don't see a need to relieve you of your duties – for now. Besides, Troke hasn't made it official. As yet, he hasn't lodged a formal complaint against you. So you get on with the case and leave this little irritation to me. There's a couple of things I'll try."

"OK," Brett agreed. "Thanks."

His superior officer wheezed, "Don't thank me till I deliver."

Brett leant against the comical tortoise and sighed. Below him, a train scampered out of the tunnel on its journey towards Sheffield and rushed past Edale without stopping. Brett looked at his watch for the fifth time. It was 4.20pm. Zoe was late and his apprehension was mounting. High on the Peaks, it was breezy, but not unpleasant. If he felt cold, it was nothing to do with the weather. The wind disturbed his hair and loose jacket. He looked towards Upper Needless and wondered if something had happened to Zoe. He could easily envisage Thomas locking her in her room if he discovered that she had arranged to meet him.

The serenity of the Horsehill Tor was shattered by a low-flying military aircraft. It was so close that Brett could imagine raising his arm and touching its undercarriage. He grimaced until distance and the wind banished the ugly roar of its engines. Brett checked the time – 4.28. He would give her two more minutes and then he would sneak into the village to find her in case she had got into trouble. Down in the valley near the camp site, a car pulling a caravan sounded its horn twice before it tackled an acute bend in the road. To Brett, it looked like a model on a child's layout and the horn was barely audible.

Half-past four. Brett scanned the uplands for the best route down to Upper Needless – for any route down to Upper Needless. Before he spotted a likely course, he spotted Zoe. She was hurrying towards him along the ridge, her hair streaming behind her. She was wearing jeans and a home-made top. Not even out of breath, she was agile across the rough terrain. She belonged to the hillside as much as the mountain sheep did.

Brett walked towards her. His relief went beyond a police officer's satisfaction at the appearance of a possible witness. "Hi," he greeted her. "Are you OK?"

She looked anxious. "Sorry. Thought I might have missed you. I got held up."

Brett examined her face and asked, "Meaning?"

She shrugged as if to dismiss the issue as trivial. Even so, she explained, "There was a meeting in the hall after school. Uncle Thomas wanted to remind all the youngsters about their duty to the village and warn them about mixing with strangers. Of course, his lecture was directed at me, really."

"But you still came," Brett said. "I appreciate it. I hope I won't land you in any more bother."

"He told me not to see you again, but…" Glancing around, Zoe smiled ruefully. "Can't see anyone following me. He won't find out." Beneath her casual demeanour, she seemed to be troubled.

Together they strolled to the tortoise head and stood behind it, using the rock as a windbreak. They looked at each other like kids about to do something naughty, wondering at the last minute if they dared.

"Well," Brett said, "I guess I ought to ask you again if you know anything about the murder victims."

Zoe's expression changed drastically. She turned away from Brett and stared into the valley, trying to derive some comfort from one of her favourite sights. Without looking at Brett, she nodded. "You know I do. You've always known. That's why you want to keep seeing me."

"It's not the only reason," Brett insisted, but he said no more because he did not want to change the subject. He wanted to get it over with. He wanted to be the detached professional police officer before he became anything else to her.

Still Zoe was silent, gazing over the myriad shades of green. Her profile betrayed her grief as well as her beauty.

Brett went to her side and plucked the picture of Victim Number Two from his jacket pocket. "Does it help if I ask you if this is a likeness of a young woman from Upper Needless who once had an accident with a scythe?" He held it in front of her. "A young woman called Emma who had a baby three months ago."

It was like watching a snowman melt under a ferocious sun. Zoe did not crumple physically but emotionally. It was just as pitiful. Abject misery destroyed her good looks. She put her hands over her face and she heaved with unrestrained sobs.

Brett was trained not to show sympathy until he had extracted all of the information that he needed.

He was supposed to let her torment work for him. Actually, he was aching to touch her, to hold her, but he resisted the temptation to offer solace.

"She was my friend," Zoe admitted. Three months of pretence fell away and her face streamed. She forced out the words slowly and painfully. "Emma Haines. It started this time last year." Her voice was hushed, croaky. Sometimes mixed with her weeping, she choked over her words. "She was seeing this lad from Castleton."

"Rob Troke?"

Zoe's red eyes darted to Brett. "Rob, yes. I never knew his other name." She looked away and stammered. "She made a fool of herself. Thought Rob loved her. But he was an outsider, just having fun at her expense. The men caught him and taught him a lesson. Emma was disgraced in the eyes of the village. I suppose, when she had the baby, she must have gone to show him to Rob. Her last attempt to win him back. Her last anything," she blurted.

"Why didn't you say anything before?" Brett enquired softly.

In a forlorn attempt to stem the flow, Zoe wiped her eyes and mouth. "Uncle Thomas wouldn't allow it. If we'd have told you who they were, he said you'd be all over the village, prying into this and that, corrupting our way of life. Said you'd destroy us."

"I still don't understand," Brett admitted. "What about her parents? Why didn't *they* report her missing?"

"You have to see it from their point of view," she cried. "Emma was in disgrace. They disowned her. As far as they were concerned, they didn't have a daughter."

Brett could see it all too easily. He knew the destructive capability of grudges between parents and offspring. As Brett thought about it, sadness threatened to overwhelm him so he tried to distance himself by continuing the questioning. "*Did* she ever have an accident with a scythe?" he asked.

"Is it important?"

"Only to the police. For identification."

"It was ages ago. A nasty cut on her leg when she was working on the farm."

"I've got to ask you about the other victims," Brett said regretfully.

Zoe coughed and sighed. "I know. Paul started it all, really. Paul Morrod. He was restless, I suppose, and that began a sort of mini-rebellion in some of the youngsters. Like Emma. She wanted more than Upper Needless. She wanted Rob. Paul wanted freedom to play tennis. He was a terrific player. You should have seen him," she sobbed. "The power and precision. He could hit the ball anywhere at any speed. Superb."

Interrupting, Brett asked, "Was he left-handed?"

"Yes, he was. How did you know that?"

"Our pathologist reported strong bones in the left arm of one of the victims."

Zoe mumbled, "Oh. Well, perhaps you've seen our

tennis court. Hardly worthy of the name. To practise and get himself known, he tried to join a Sheffield tennis club." She broke down again. When she was able to continue, she muttered, "Uncle Thomas is right. When we mix with outsiders, it's a recipe for disaster. We end up dead." She turned and looked directly, meaningfully, at Brett.

Brett saw anguish and remorse in Zoe's white face. He realized that she was anticipating the worst by consorting with him. He also realized that she was summoning every last bit of her courage to talk to him.

"We all swear an oath of allegiance to the village," she informed him. "Paul broke it by wanting to leave and further his tennis."

"So he was disgraced as well," Brett reasoned. "What happened to him?"

"One day he just disappeared," she whispered. "It was a year ago. We'd tried to put him out of our minds. Then you and your people came round asking questions."

"Did Paul take part in the punishment dished out to Rob Troke, or had he already gone by then?"

"No. He was still around – just – but I don't know if he was involved," Zoe answered.

"The other victim," Brett prompted. "The boy."

"Lewis Simmonds. You know," Zoe said, "your picture of Emma was pretty close. Enough to upset me. I wouldn't have recognized Paul from his picture, but you got Lewis spot on. I don't want to know how you did it. It's uncanny, frightening. You brought him back to life!"

Zoe began to cry uncontrollably. She was almost dissolving in her own tears. Suddenly, Brett's role of police officer became unimportant. The woman in front of him needed a friend. He could not resist that need. He wasn't superhuman and he wasn't cruel. Irresistibly, he took her in his arms and hugged her.

In return, she clasped him like a drowning woman clinging to a buoy. If it had not been for Brett she would have collapsed.

After a full minute, Brett felt her pull away slightly. She looked up into his face with an imploring expression. He bent his head and kissed her fully, passionately. She clutched him even harder.

Five minutes later, he could not believe what he had done. In the midst of Zoe's distress, he had made a pass at her. Just when she was at her most vulnerable, he had kissed her. It had seemed the natural thing to do; unthinkingly, he had done it. He had abandoned himself to instinct, not even considering that she was a vital witness in a murder case. He had taken advantage of her in her moment of weakness. He felt like a teacher who had abused the trust of a student, yet when she held him, he could not help himself. He thought – and hoped – that Zoe was gaining more than comfort from him. He put his hand on the back of her head and savoured the softness of her hair between his fingers. His heart pounded pleasurably. He felt privileged.

And irresponsible.

It was supposed to be a day for steering clear of trouble. Already he had been accused of beating a suspect, questioned a woman about his own chief superintendent, and now he had fallen for a witness. He was living up to his name all right. Even deluged by misgivings, he could not deny the fact that it felt wonderful to embrace her.

Zoe disentangled herself, kissed him gently on the lips, and murmured, "I can go on now, if you like."

Brett was torn. If he had not controlled his own feelings, he would have cried as well. He marvelled at her bravery and tenacity. "If you want to, yes."

More composed, she continued, "Lewis was just a kid. A bit backward. He didn't have the intelligence to rebel. He was just following in Paul's footsteps. He pretended he was playing football for a youth team in Castleton. He wasn't. He just followed them around. A supporter. No doubt, an unwanted one. I bet they laughed at him. The village idiot."

"Yes," Brett murmured knowingly to himself. He was remembering that the squad had been told of a missing supporter but had dismissed the report because the lad's absence didn't coincide with the initial date of Victim Number Four's murder. Brett asked, "Lewis disappeared as well?" Seeing her nod, he enquired, "When?"

She dabbed her eyes with a handkerchief while she thought about it. "Just after the New Year. First game in January, I guess."

"Do you know the name of the team?"

She shook her head.

Brett took her hand. Without thinking, he expected her hands to be smooth and soft, but they were the hands of a manual worker. Not much smaller than his own, her right hand was hard and rough. The skin was thick and the nails short and uneven. She did not wear rings or a bracelet. He led her to a convenient rock and sat her down. "You need a rest," he counselled. Squatting in front of her, he began, "You've been —" Abruptly, he stopped himself. He wanted to tell her how courageous and helpful she had been, but it would have sounded too cold and officious. It would have been Detective Inspector Lawless speaking. He wanted to tell her how attractive and desirable she was, but it would have sounded too presumptuous and emotional. It would have been Brett's sentimentality gushing. Instead, he remarked, "It's taken it out of you."

Zoe looked into Brett's face and said, "When I was small, I used to take clocks apart. You know — to see how they worked. I got into trouble for it more than once." Zoe shook her head at the memory. "When I put them back together, they used to go all right but there were always a few bits left over that didn't seem to fit anywhere. A couple of tiny screws or a small cog. That's how I think of Emma, Paul and Lewis. They weren't part of Upper Needless any more. The village went on all right and they didn't have a place in it. But, deep down, we all knew something was missing – that some day it could all go wrong. The missing bits would make Upper Needless grind to a halt." Utterly drained, she sighed loudly. Then, suddenly and desperately, she asked, "Now you've got what you want from me, will I see you again?"

Brett was startled that such a thought should occur to her. "How can you say that after…?" he exclaimed. He let out his feelings after all. "I needed the information, sure. But I want *you*," he stressed. He allowed her to gaze into his face and see his honesty.

She flung her arms round his neck. "Good," she whispered in his ear.

Tentatively, Brett said, "Really, I should come into the village to speak to your uncle and the families."

Horrified, Zoe sat back from him. "You can't do that. Please!"

Brett nodded at her. "I know. Thomas would put two and two together and realize that I'd got this information from you. Then you'd be in more trouble. I don't want that. I'll have to drop that line of questioning."

"Promise?" Zoe urged.

"Promise." Sitting next to her and putting his arm across her shoulders, he commented, "I hate to say it, but you've been away a while. When you're ready, perhaps I ought to walk you back."

"No!" she exclaimed. "I have to go on my own. Remember Uncle Thomas's ban. I mustn't be seen with you."

Brett sighed. "OK. If you're certain you'll be all right on your own."

"This is my home," she replied, indicating the upland scenery. "This is where I feel best."

"Would you feel good here again tomorrow? Same time, same place?"

"Yes. But not tomorrow," Zoe replied. "It's too soon. Too suspicious."

"The day after?"

"I'll be here. But," she added, "why don't we have a few more minutes right now?"

Brett smiled impudently, trying to lift her spirits. "Good idea."

14

After his encounter with Zoe, Brett was unable to face his colleagues in the incident room. Emotionally, he felt exhausted. By morning, though, he was eager to share his findings. He cut short his run and got to work early. By the time that the rest of the squad had arrived and transformed the ghostly room into a bawdy hive of activity, Brett had transformed the patchy whiteboard into a tapestry of information about the victims. Most importantly, he had discovered the link between them. At last, there was a logic to the murders. The team had a motive to direct its investigation. Hatred of the young people of Upper Needless.

In making the breakthrough that the team craved, Brett also transformed his colleagues' opinions of him. The whole atmosphere in the incident room changed. It became upbeat and cordial.

Brett's list of suspects on the whiteboard was not complete. He had omitted Keith and Rebecca Johnstone for the sake of diplomacy. Occupying pride of place on the list was Rob Troke, beaten up by a gang from Upper Needless and apparently with a contempt for Emma and his own child. His brother, Glenn Troke, was also accorded a place in the rogues' gallery but it was not so prominent. George Bottomley was still a suspect, particularly if he had found the youngsters near his land and thought that they were going to steal his sheep. Andrew Smith and his lover, Julie Penny, were also suspects. The investigation had started with them, had not really ruled them out, and yet none of the new facts incriminated them further. It was still possible that the investigation might end with them, though.

Big John had already contacted colleagues in London. Later, they would ransack Rob Troke's flat for signs of a firearm. For now, Rob was speeding north up the M1 in a police car. "Serious questioning called for," John announced with glee. "But," he said to Brett, "you're dropped. Given the state of play between you and our chief suspect's brother, a bias in questioning would be claimed later. That would screw up our entire case if he is our man."

Frustrated at missing the juiciest interview so far, Brett turned to Greg. "Any joy with that solicitor handling the Upper Needless inheritance?"

More co-operative than previously, Greg replied, "Nothing yet. Still checking."

Intervening, John said, "If you want to continue with that angle, Brett, you do it. I need Greg to organize a search of the Trokes' place in Castleton. I've got a warrant to turn it inside out for a gun. Again, you can't take part. A defence lawyer would have a field day if you found a weapon in the house where he'd lived, just before his brother lodged a complaint against you. These days, juries *will* believe that we plant evidence on people."

Brett felt that he was being shunted on to a branchline. He understood the reason for it but it irritated him. Even so, he would not be sitting nervously outside the interview room like a squeamish would-be father waiting for a reluctant new arrival. There were still things to be done. There were further questions that he wanted to ask Zoe. Yesterday, he believed, he'd put her through enough without pestering her to recall the exact dates of the victims' disappearances, their clothing at the time and a hundred other details. He would plan out his questions for tomorrow.

Before his concentration was broken by day-dreams of Zoe, he quickly turned to Greg's file. Basically, it was a list of solicitors and their telephone numbers, in which most of the entries had been crossed out. Greg had contacted all of the firms in the obvious catchment area of the Vale of Edale, Hathersage and Sheffield. Only a few outlying places remained. Brett sighed. He realized that he should have asked Zoe another question. He should have discovered where the generous Matthew Robinson had lived before he went to Upper Needless. Maybe his solicitor was near his previous address. But surely, Brett thought, he would have decided to leave his estate to Upper Needless once he had taken up residence there. It made sense that his solicitor would be nearby.

Suddenly Brett sat upright. He grabbed a road atlas and studied a small-scale map of northern England. "Interesting," he uttered to himself. Sheffield was not quite the nearest large conurbation to Edale. Macclesfield was slightly closer. It was perfectly possible that Matthew Robinson had gone west rather than east to find a solicitor. As soon as Brett had come up with the idea, he was struck by the prospect of another connection. Julie Penny was a solicitor in Macclesfield. Her lover, Andrew Smith, knew all about money. If Robinson had hired Penny, Gallup and Tomlinson Solicitors to handle his bequest, Penny and Smith could now be cheating both their dead client and the village out of their legacy, somehow taking a share of the spoils for themselves. He called out to Liz, still perched in front of a computer screen, "Can you tell me if either Julie Penny or Andrew Smith – or both – were in Edale at the new time of Lewis Simmonds's death? Any time in January." Even if the Penny, Gallup and Tomlinson firm had been hired by Matthew Robinson all those years ago and if Julie Penny was creaming off some of the bequest, Brett could not see an association with the murders. Still, he was keen to establish whether there was a new connection between Upper Needless and the two suspects in Macclesfield. He scanned his own notes for the telephone number of her firm.

Liz called out, "No. I can't say they weren't there, but we've got no information that they were."

"Thanks," Brett replied, somewhat disappointed.

Then he remembered something. He continued to check his notes of the interview with Mrs Penny. He was right. She'd said that she had a client near Edale and that she visited that person every January. It was a day trip so her name would never appear on any hotel lists, but *she* had been in the area when Lewis Simmonds had been killed. Brett began to believe that he could be on to something.

He picked up the telephone and called Penny, Gallup and Tomlinson Solicitors. He was put through to a junior partner because Mrs Penny was out seeing a client. Brett was delighted. If Julie Penny was guilty of fraud, she would not admit to Brett that she was dealing with the will. He would only have got a truthful response from her if she had been acting legitimately. A junior partner would simply give him the facts.

"A Matthew Robinson of Upper Needless, you say?" The solicitor muttered incoherently as he tried to recall contracts or studied records. "You'll have to speak to Mrs Penny, really, but I do seem to recall such a trust fund. Upper Needless – not a name that's easily forgotten," he mumbled. "And it's old, you say. Probably originally taken on by Mrs Penny's dear departed grandfather, Edward Tomlinson." He paused and Brett thought that he heard the sound of tapping at a keyboard. "Yes," the solicitor proclaimed. "I can't give you much in the way of details for the sake of confidentiality but the Robinson legacy is still an active file."

"Active, even now?"

"Yes," he replied, plainly unwilling to divulge more information.

"What else can you tell me – without upsetting your deceased client?"

"Can you fax to me a signed confirmation of who you say you are on official notepaper and a request for information on behalf of the police force? So I can check your credentials. With all due respect, you could be anyone."

"Hold the line," Brett said, snatching up a piece of headed notepaper. "I'll do it staightaway." He jotted a formal enquiry regarding Matthew Robinson's will, signed it and faxed it immediately.

At the other end of the line, the solicitor said, "OK. Something's coming through. The wonders of modern technology. Hold on a moment." Again he muttered to himself for a while. Then he stated, "That all seems to be in order, Detective Inspector Lawless. Now, I'm still not prepared to go into details and amounts. Mrs Penny will have to decide if that's appropriate or not, but I can say this: Mr Robinson left a sizeable lump sum to the village of Upper Needless. A proportion of it was donated with immediate effect. The bulk went into a trust fund that provides Upper Needless with a substantial figure each year. There were no restrictions on how it was to be used and successive village elders were made responsible for it. However, there were two conditions laid down for the continuation of the bequest. Obviously, Mr Robinson wished to ensure that his haven remained unspoilt. The rustic character of the village should not change. In a nut-shell, that's the first condition. Second, the young people of Upper Needless should remain in the village and help to preserve its gentle way of life. If you ask me," the solicitor mused, "they've been required to swim against a strong tide. I don't like computers but I had to surrender to progress. Now I've got three of the damn things. Can't get by without them. Anyway," he said, returning to the point, "so far, the two stipulations have been met. Upper Needless seems to be putting up a brave fight against the onslaught of new technology. Good for them, I say. Long may their defiance continue."

"I see," Brett replied, his spine tingling as it used to in a biochemistry lab when an experiment made everything clear. He always experienced a great thrill when the pieces came together and the whole began to make perfect sense. "So, one reason the file's still active is because someone has to go to Upper Needless periodically and make sure that the villagers are adhering to Mr Robinson's intentions?"

"Mrs Penny makes an annual trip."

"And if they weren't, the money would be forfeited?"

"Indeed."

"Thank you," he said. "Thank you very much. I don't need further details so I won't need to contact Mrs Penny. You've been most helpful."

Brett put down the receiver and shouted, "Yes!" He called to Liz, "Is your computer clever enough to have a database of people who have firearm licences?"

"No," Liz shouted back. "But it's networked to one that does. It'll take me a couple of minutes."

"OK. Check out Julie Penny of 14 Cedar Way, Macclesfield for me. Bet she's on the list."

Big John crashed into the room like a charging rhinoceros. He bellowed at Brett, "I've just been interrupted. Pulled out of the interview, much to my annoyance. Rob Troke's violent, unstable and screwy. Almost certainly the baby's father. At last, I've got me a real candidate. I need to dedicate myself to questioning him. And what happens? The Chief summons me to talk about you. *You!* Seems you've been breaking rank. Your grip on this case is rather tenuous. In fact, forget that. Your grip on your *job's* rather tenuous." He reached the point where he would either explode or deflate like a balloon. Unaccustomed to exertion, he seemed exhausted and opted for the latter. "I stopped him going ballistic –

just. Only because you've advanced the investigation so much by discovering the identities of the bodies. But," he sighed, "why did you choose to check on his movements through one of his faithful country chums? Word was bound to get back to him. It was stupid at best."

"I wasn't to know the hotel manageress was his friend," Brett explained. "So, what's going to happen to me?"

His commanding officer shrugged. "To be decided. Disobeying an order doesn't go down too well around here."

"You know why I did it. It had to be done."

Big John had vented most of his anger and was calming down. He dabbed at his glistening forehead with a handkerchief as if he were waving a white flag. "I also warned you what would happen. Luckily, you've moved us two paces forward and only one back. You're still in credit."

"But if Glenn Troke pursues his claim against me, that's my credit gone?"

"It would be, yes, but after he spoke to the officer I sent out there this morning, he's dropping it," John informed him.

"Oh. Why?" Brett asked, surprised that the threat had been removed so abruptly. "What was your angle?"

"One: Glenn Troke was told that if he made a formal complaint, we'd get our specialists to study his wound. He was informed that it was simple to distinguish a wound made by a fist from anything else. A rock, say. Two: he was reminded that the attendant at Peak Cavern overlooked the scene of the purported thumping."

"And did he see anything?" Brett enquired.

"There are some questions best not asked," John replied. "The fact is that Troke, thinking it'd be his word against two and a discredited wound, has backed off."

"Well," Brett responded, "you delivered, so now's the time to thank you."

"Now's the time *you'd* better keep delivering if I'm going to stop disciplinary measures – or at least minimize them," John said. "Though it grieves me to say it – and I never thought I would – I want to keep you on this case."

Brett smiled. "Thanks. I think I can deliver something big tomorrow. I need another solo outing to get more out of my Upper Needless mole." He hated to refer to Zoe coldly like that but if he showed any affection towards her, it would be several paces backwards. "I think we've been barking up the wrong tree altogether."

Big John was intrigued but he said, "OK. Don't tell me about it now. Work on it and come back to me if there's anything in it. I give you a free hand, but don't abuse it again. Right now, my chief suspect's waiting anxiously for me. I need to crack him before his lawyer starts playing tricks."

He turned and shuffled away at his normal pace –

a rhinoceros in labour. Brett turned to Liz and asked, "Well?"

She smiled at him. "Clever boy! You were right. She's licensed to keep a thirty-eight."

Brett walked purposefully across the incident room and, on his list of suspects, underlined the name of Julie Penny in red.

That night, Brett spent a long time in his front room with the aquarium lamp as the only source of light. It could make the lounge seem eerie or soothing, depending on his mood. This evening, whenever the discus fish shifted, the patterns of shadow and light shifted uncannily, exaggerating the movement in the aquarium. He watched the isolated community in the corner of his own living room, realizing that it had its own secrets that he, an outsider, would never understand. It was attractive and fascinating but, no matter how long he observed it, he would always be excluded from its intimate relationships. He would never really know what the small dashing guppies, yellow labidochromis, tetras and lyretail silver mollies thought of sharing their high-speed world with a bulky and placid discus with its blue and brown markings like the map of a maze.

He was looking forward to seeing Zoe again, but he wished that she was free of the investigation, rather than at its centre. He comforted himself with the thought that he had only one more question for her. He would not have to take her to the edge again.

15

It was a stifling day. Breathless. Brett returned from his run, saturated with sweat. Later, in the Vale of Edale, it was just as suffocating. The air was still and clammy. Death Valley.

He was early for his tryst with Zoe. He sat down, his back against the angry old man with the protruding nose, and kept watch over the valley. He was so consumed by his own chaotic thoughts that he did not hear the three lads from Upper Needless approaching him. When they appeared at his side, Brett jumped a little and banged his head on the rock.

"You're the policeman," one of them stated impassively.

"Not today," Brett lied. He rubbed the back of his head before adding, "Today, I'm a tourist."

"You're off the beaten track. No one comes up here. The Pennine Way's over there," the young man said, pointing over the crest of Broadlee-bank Tor towards the camp site beyond Edale. The lad's tone suggested that he should move on.

"I like it here," Brett assured them. "More peaceful than the Pennine Way." He was wary of the youngsters but did not feel threatened. He knew that Rob Troke had been lynched by a mob for befriending Emma Haines, but attacking a police officer was a different matter, even if they had found out that he was meeting Zoe. Brett was more concerned for Zoe than he was for himself. Besides, he was confident that he could defend himself against three lads – unless, of course, they had weapons. Examining them, he saw no worrying bulges in their clothing. He also noticed that the smallest of the three looked very uncomfortable. He did not relish the confrontation. The trio did not make a particularly convincing punishment gang.

"Are you sure you're not here on business?" asked the tallest of them, as if he could dictate Brett's behaviour.

"Do I look as if I'm working?" Brett replied, still slouching against the rock. He looked round theatrically and commented, "Apart from yourselves, I don't see anyone to arrest. Do you?"

They scowled at him, recognizing that he was baiting them. "What are you really doing here?" one of them snapped.

Brett decided to remain civil. "Enjoying the air, the view, the peace and quiet. For a townie like me, it's a real pleasure." He looked at his watch. Fifteen minutes before Zoe was due. "And," he added with a grin, "I guarantee it's perfectly legal."

"Have you caught anyone for those murders?"

"No. Not yet."

"You shouldn't be lolling about, then, because you've obviously got plenty of work to do."

Brett's patience was wearing thin. He got to his feet declaring, "I don't need your advice on how to do my job but you're right about one thing. It's time I moved on." He reckoned that walking away was the best means of shaking them off. As he set out along the ridge, he could not resist saying over his shoulder, "Thanks for making me so welcome here."

Brett did not have to look back to realize that the boys from Upper Needless remained by the rocks, watching him until he was out of their sight. Once well away from them, he stopped in a secluded spot, sat on another rock, and sighed. He decided not to return to the meeting place for at least ten minutes to give them time to retreat.

He hoped that, back at headquarters, Rob Troke was pouring out his heart – and his confession – to Detective Superintendent Macfarlane. Brett hoped that, as far as police work was concerned, he was wasting his time. He wanted to meet Zoe for the sole reason that he found her immensely attractive. Yet he doubted that he would be allowed that luxury. In carrying out his duty to catch a killer, he was well aware that he could put Zoe at considerable risk. He hated what he was doing.

He nearly jumped out of his skin when someone tapped him on the shoulder. He turned to see Zoe with a forefinger on her lips. She whispered, "It's amazing how sound travels up here on a still day. It's too dangerous. Follow me."

Quietly and unquestioningly, Brett got to his feet and followed her down the hillside, away from their intended meeting place. In her element, she moved effortlessly and smoothly. Sometimes, she had to slow down to allow Brett to catch up with her. She led him over Cowburn Tunnel and below the tree line. At Dalehead, she took him into a spinney, just like the crude burial ground that was about a mile further along the rail track. Inside the small wood, they could have been on a different planet. At least it was shady and cool.

Zoe halted and turned towards him. Brett did not stop walking till he was wrapped in her arms. Hugging her, he could forget the bodies, the investigation, his credit that was slipping away rapidly. When they next looked into each other's exhilarated faces, they both understood that they were sharing something extraordinary. Without putting it into words, they knew that they were indulging themselves in more than a passing infatuation. They kissed.

Withdrawing from his embrace but keeping his

hand in hers, Zoe uttered, "It's almost frightening."

Brett realized that she was talking about the intensity of their sudden relationship. He nodded. "Frightening – but good?"

She smiled. "Very good." She leaned against a tree, silently inviting him to hold her again.

Happily, he obliged.

They were so quiet and still that a squirrel scuttled across the wood and nearly ran into them. Just a short distance away, it froze when it realized that they were human beings. After a few seconds it turned and bounded away with its sleek grey tail bobbing behind it. Deftly and swiftly, it scaled the trunk of a tree. Neither Brett nor Zoe noticed it. "When do you need to get back?" Brett asked her, dreading the response.

Zoe shrugged. "Well before nightfall. No one sane takes a walk here after dark. If I got back late, Uncle Thomas would know something was going on."

Brett was reminded of his mid-teenage years when dating a girl became the art of hoodwinking the parents – the enemy. He thought that he'd left those days behind but apparently he hadn't. Despite their ages, Zoe and Brett had to deceive her uncle. They both believed that there was more at stake than an argument and a grounding. Upper Needless inhabitants who consorted with outsiders seemed to end up dead.

"Your uncle," Brett said, "he's pretty stern."

"He's kind and caring. He cares passionately about

the village, the people and its way of life. Sometimes he's overprotective. That's why he might seem stern."

"Seems to me he rules the village like a tyrant."

Zoe's expression indicated sad agreement more than denial. "He's sweet most of the time, nice as anything, like a dad to me, but he can change suddenly. He starts to rave about God's will. He does it when he thinks the village is under threat. It's insecurity, I guess. He thinks it's the best way to keep Upper Needless going. I don't know." She sighed then added, "But I hope you haven't come to talk about Uncle Thomas."

"No. But I do have to ask you something."

"Oh." Disgruntled, Zoe grumbled, "You've become a police officer again."

Brett nodded. "I can't help it, Zoe. I'm sorry but I have to get to the bottom of it." He held her and enquired, "What do you know about Julie Penny?"

Zoe looked surprised. "She's some sort of solicitor. Comes here and talks to Uncle Thomas."

"Do you know what about?"

"Yes. It's about our inheritance from Matthew Robinson. She makes sure the village carries on like he would've wanted it to."

"Does she just breeze in and out, or does she take it seriously?"

"Now you mention it," Zoe answered, "she takes quite a bit of interest. She bought one of my sketches once. Anyway, I think she's supposed to come at the start of each year but I've seen her here at other times as well. She comes to the house to talk to Uncle Thomas. Asking all about life in the village. She's pretty thorough."

Brett nodded slowly. "I thought she might be. Do you know if she found out about Emma, Paul and Lewis? Did she know they got a bit restless?"

"I don't know. Possibly. Why?"

"Well," Brett began, seeing no reason to hide his latest theory from her. "What if Julie Penny was taking some of the Upper Needless inheritance for herself?" He put his hands on Zoe's shoulders as he explained. "She'd have a vested interest in making sure that the village kept on the straight and narrow. She wouldn't want Emma, Paul or Lewis to spoil her little scam. She'd want Upper Needless to qualify for the legacy for as long as possible. Then she could hand over a portion of the money to your uncle each year and keep a fair bit for herself. You might be entitled to a lot more than you get."

Zoe looked up at him and said, "You mean, she'd kill to stop the village changing?"

"It's a real possibility," he replied.

"That's horrible!"

"Yes," Brett agreed.

"But," Zoe objected, "even if the village did modernize, she could just cheat. She could swear the village wasn't changing, keep giving us the money – or some of it – and keep the rest to herself."

"I don't think she'd do that," Brett replied. "It'd be

too easy to get caught. Sometime, one of her partners might do the inspection. Sooner or later, she'd retire from the job and then she'd be found out."

Zoe nodded. "I see what you mean."

"I have to go and see her, Zoe. Check it out."

"Now?"

"Not immediately and not on my own," Brett answered her. He did not tell her that, before he visited such a potentially dangerous suspect, he would probably have to be armed.

"You be careful," Zoe said, hugging him.

Brett did not say so, but he was more concerned for Zoe's safety. If, somehow, Julie Penny discovered that Zoe had started a relationship with him, the solicitor would regard it as a threat to the village. A threat to her income. And, if Brett was right, he knew how ruthlessly she dealt with threats.

"You'd best be getting home." Brett kissed her ardently, as if for the last time.

Breathlessly, she said, "Yes. I suppose we'd both better be making tracks."

"I'll walk with you as far as…"

Putting a finger on his lips, she interrupted him. "No. I need to walk out of here on my own. Just in case the lads are still around." Sadly, she added, "You wouldn't want it getting around that we're … you know."

"True," Brett admitted.

"You wait here for a few minutes then go straight to your car."

Brett muttered, "Isn't the police officer the one who's supposed to dish out the orders?"

"Not in this relationship," she replied. "Take care," she repeated and then she walked away. Before she disappeared between the trees she turned and, completely naturally, called, "Bye, love."

Brett raised his hand in reply. He watched her until the countryside claimed her and then he leant against a trunk. His heart was pounding. No one, not even his parents, had ever called him "love". And now a marvellous, matchless woman had done so, even after he had tortured her. He felt the impulse to give in to his emotions while he was on his own. But he fought against it. He did not allow himself the indulgence. He was a man and a police officer.

He drove back to headquarters at speed. The incident room was full of frustrated faces. As soon as Brett walked into the room, Big John brought him up to date. "We've got problems with our favourite suspect, Rob Troke. He's nasty. He despises the people of Upper Needless. He's a time-bomb waiting to go off. And that's the problem. I don't think he *has* exploded yet. And we haven't had a sniff of a weapon at either house. I don't think he's our man."

"Neither do I," Brett agreed.

"What?" Big John exclaimed.

"Neither do I," Brett repeated.

All of the officers in the incident room stopped what they were doing and watched Brett.

"Why do you say that?" John enquired.

Brett pointed to the whiteboard where he had underlined Julie Penny's name. "There's my chief suspect."

The room was totally silent for the first time. A vacuum waiting for Brett to fill it. He did not have to be asked. He told them his latest theory and the facts that lay behind it. She was on the scene at the time of each murder. And while she was there she used aliases – apparently not just in case of an inquisitive husband. She owned the right type of weapon. She'd taken a substantial interest in Upper Needless and its inhabitants. There was a likely motive. "As a serial killer, she'd be a cleaner, I guess," Brett concluded. "Ridding Upper Needless of its radicals for her own profit."

"OK," John declared after he'd heard his assistant. "It's enough to question her again, look into her bank balance and confiscate her gun for tests. The trouble is," he said, looking at his watch, "it's going to take time to get over to Macclesfield. I'll get on to Cheshire Constabulary," he decided. "Request that they send in an armed response pronto."

Slowly the room emptied as the evening turned to dusk. Eventually, only John, Brett, Clare and Liz remained, surrounded by empty plastic cups. They were too edgy for conversation or banter. The room was nervously silent. The telephone refused steadfastly to ring with news from Macclesfield.

Isolated from the action on the other side of the Pennines, Brett felt frustrated. It didn't seem right to gather the facts, formulate a theory and then hand it over to someone else to test. He would have preferred to see it through himself. He couldn't even be a spectator. He could only imagine the armed officers surrounding Julie Penny's house, taking every precaution until they had separated the suspect from her weapon. Glancing at the telephone, he willed an incoming call.

Big John groaned loudly as he pushed himself out of his chair. "More coffee anyone?"

"All right," they all murmured together. They didn't need another drink – they didn't even want it – but it passed the time. Drinking was something to do while they waited anxiously.

When the phone eventually rang, it sounded as loud as an alarm and Brett jolted, spilling a little of his coffee. They all looked to John who rose painfully slowly from his seat. Picking up the receiver, he muttered, "Yes?"

There were a few seconds of silence and then he responded, "Yes."

An agonizing minute passed before John said, "Are you sure? Did you go over the place?"

Almost immediately, he asked, "Which hotel? Do you know?"

They could tell by the look on the Detective Chief Inspector's face and his terse responses that something was not to his liking. To confirm it, he cursed into the handset. Then he said, "Thanks anyway. It's back in our court now. I can take it from here. Cheers." He put down the telephone.

To his impatient audience, he said, "After all that, she's not there. According to her husband, she left for Edale earlier. And, before you ask, no, he didn't know where she was staying. A guest house or hotel. That's all he knew."

"Did they search for her gun?" asked Clare.

"Didn't need to. Her husband told them she takes it with her. A lawyer needs to defend herself, he said, if any clients turn nasty."

"And it's no use trying to trace her through the hotels," Brett moaned. "She uses different names each time she goes." He stared at the ceiling in horror. What if the boys on Horsehill Tor had seen Zoe with him? What if Julie Penny had already been to Upper Needless and heard rumours about Zoe? Brett thought that he had left Zoe safely at home but she could be in real danger.

"Now what?" Liz asked.

"We call Keith Johnstone in. We can't do much without his say so." John reached for the phone again.

Brett groaned. Yet more delay. "But Zoe Adamson could be in trouble if she was seen talking to me."

"Yes," John replied. "I *had* figured that out for myself. But all I can do is despatch an unarmed copper. He can keep watch on the house and alert us if Julie Penny turns up. OK?"

Brett shrugged. An inadequate response seemed to be the only response possible. It was better than nothing. "OK," he agreed.

Half an hour later, Brett was standing in front of Detective Chief Superintendent Keith Johnstone with Big John and again he had to narrate his story and justify the arrest that he wished to make.

"OK," Keith pronounced. "I've heard enough. I'm authorizing the issue of firearms. I'll call Diana in. You'll get your smart guns tonight."

"Make it tomorrow," John responded. "We'll set out early, to be in place by dawn."

"But we ought to get it over with straightaway," Brett argued. "You never know what Julie Penny might do between now and tomorrow."

"Look," Big John said with authority. "If there's got to be guns, I want daylight as well. I want to be able to see what we're doing and what our suspect's doing."

Keith accepted John's wisdom. "Fair enough. Dawn it is. I'll take care of Diana. You two plan the arrest. It won't be easy if you don't know exactly where she is."

Brett said, "Sooner or later she'll turn up at Adamson's house, if she's not there already."

"OK, that's good. You've got a focus. I only want two of you armed. Let's not turn it into a battlefield out there. You know what the press will make of it if there's a siege and guns blazing from all angles.

You'll get all the back-up you need but I won't sanction any more weapons. OK?"

"Suits me," John responded. "It's bad enough facing a suspect with a gun without having another twenty behind my back."

The Chief peered at Brett and said, "Remember your training. Use of firearms is warranted *only* when loss of life cannot be prevented by any other means. Got that?"

"Yes," Brett barked like a schoolboy replying to a teacher who had just recited a rule unnecessarily for the hundredth time.

"I've got great hopes for you, Brett. Given you plenty of opportunity. Invested a lot in you." Keith paused before adding, "Given you the benefit of the doubt. Don't make me regret it."

The doubt, Brett knew, was a reference to his illicit investigation of the Johnstones. The Chief was still staring intently at him when he replied, "No, sir. I won't."

The tetras, guppies and silver mollies in Brett's aquarium never seemed to sleep. That night, Brett was just as restless. In bed, he tossed and turned all night, failing to find relaxation and sleep. The sheets stuck to his perspiring body and whenever he changed position, they became even more disarrayed and uncomfortable. He got up and strolled round the house to cool down. He made the bed, clambered in and tried again. No chance. He spent the rest of the night on his back, hands clasped behind his head, gazing beyond his bedroom ceiling. He was wondering if Zoe was awake or asleep. He was wondering if she was unharmed and secure. Most of all, he could not put out of his mind her final word: love.

Brett turned on the light and prepared a simple breakfast. He did not feel like eating. He brought himself alive with a sharp fruit juice and forced himself to eat a little cereal. He did not shave or take a shower. Missing his morning run for the first time, he left the house before the sun poked above the horizon.

The city was like a ghost town, waiting for daylight and unquiet commuters to resurrect it. Brett was eager to conclude the morning's business and dreading it at the same time. He drove through the dormant streets at speed. He did not have to hurry but the emptiness of Sheffield was an invitation to assert himself. Outside headquarters, four minibuses and two police vans were drawn up in a line, like a fleet about to set sail for the war zone.

Inside, there was an expectant buzz. Everyone was anticipating daybreak and the outbreak of hostilities. Brett began to feel the excited tingle of being part of a single-minded team. He could not help being infected with the thrill of swooping on the prey. There was something strengthening about sharing a common purpose. In another way, though, he also felt alone and dispirited. He was the only officer with two goals. He was preoccupied not only with the coming arrest but also with plucking Zoe from the lion's den.

An electronics technician fiddled inside Brett's shirt, wiring him for sound. Once she was satisfied with Brett, she fastened another small remote microphone on John's clothes. "No Kevlar vests?" she queried.

"We're dealing with a head-shot killer," John explained. "The troops'll be in bullet-proof clothing but there's no point for us. If she's close enough to shoot, she'll go for the head."

Along with John, Brett was a key player. Together, they were making sure that everyone was familiar with the strategy, that everyone knew their role. Big John went over the briefing twice. He did not want any mistakes. He aimed to have the Adamson house and the village hall surrounded by the time that the sun lit the Vale of Edale – in case Penny was already inside. He described himself and Brett as the first wave because they would go into the house first. The massed ranks would be the second wave, encircling the property. Beyond them, a few select officers would orchestrate the whole show: the third wave. It included Greg, Clare, Mark, Liz and the electronics technician. They would be listening in to the action using the microphones attached to Brett and Big John, reacting to developments and passing on the appropriate orders. The fourth wave would be behind the vehicles; on the road, in case Julie Penny had yet to arrive. If she did, they'd use the vans to block her in the lane to Upper Needless. There was also a forensic team: the fifth wave. The scientists were on standby until the situation had been secured and the arrest had been made. Then, they would be on hand with their sophisticated paraphernalia, searching for firearm residues and traces of blood if the suspect confessed where the victims had been killed.

Diana arrived with the weapons and ensured that she gave John and Brett their own personalized ones. "The guns are smart," she whispered to Brett. "Make sure you are as well. I want you back in one piece."

Miraculously, the organization gelled and the operation acquired a proficiency of its own. The team took shape and they headed for the transport. "Let's get going," Big John ordered. "And remember this isn't a picnic. I've just been told by Operations that our man posted in Upper Needless missed his last radio contact, due ten minutes ago. We may have a tricky situation developing."

Among the camaraderie, the adrenalin and the

high spirits, out of everyone else's hearing Clare asked Brett, "Are you OK?"

Brett looked at her and realized that she saw the apprehension in him that no one else had spotted. "I'm fine," he fibbed.

Clare frowned. "You take care of yourself," she instructed him. She hesitated before adding with sincerity, "And Zoe."

Brett's eyebrows rose. Somehow, Clare understood exactly what he was going through. She had read the tension in his face. Brett was pleased. Maybe he was not so alone after all. He appreciated her comment. "Thanks," he murmured. "I'll try."

One of the vans was reserved for the forensic scientists and their gear. The first and third waves travelled together in the second van, packed with electronic equipment. At times on the journey, they were totally silent. Otherwise, Big John raced through the details yet again, making sure that those left in the van knew precisely what he wanted them to do under any circumstances. "When I get out there," he stressed, "listen to me carefully. Turn up the volume. I might have to whisper instructions down the wires. I don't want you saying afterwards you couldn't hear. I don't want any improvization. I want my orders followed."

The van led the convoy past George Bottomley's farm, past the wood where the case had begun, and into the lane to Upper Needless. It was still dark. They parked in the road, short of the village so that their arrival would go unnoticed. The vans and minibuses blocked the lane entirely. After disgorging most of its load of police officers, one of the minibuses headed back down the lane to conceal itself in George Bottomley's drive. There it would wait. If a car turned into the road to Upper Needless, it would emerge and trap the car between police vehicles.

In the van, Big John checked for the last time, "Everyone clear about this little outing?"

The chorus murmured, "Yes, boss."

Afterwards, Greg mumbled grudgingly, "Good luck."

Brett smiled at him. "Thanks, Greg." In his face, Brett read surly acceptance.

Brett exchanged a significant glance with Clare.

"Go outside," the electronics expert commanded them, "and talk to each other. I need to check sound levels."

Exhaling loudly, John led the way. In the damp fresh air of the coming dawn he complained, "Guns and wires. It wasn't like this in the old days."

Brett was pleased to know that someone would be eavesdropping. It was like having a guardian angel. "Can you hear us all right?" he said into the ether.

An upright thumb appeared in the dark window of the van.

"Any news of the man we posted outside the house?" John enquired.

The thumb in the window turned downwards.

Big John groaned and then muttered to Brett,

"Come on, then. Let's get the job done." He began to lumber down the lane towards the centre of Upper Needless like an unwilling tank. The troops followed them towards the centre of the village. To Brett, it felt as if he were leading a furtive mission on hostile territory. In a way, that's what he was doing.

Brett halted before the village hall. Silently, he pointed out Thomas Adamson's grand house and the hall to the leader of the second wave. Then John and Brett waited impatiently for the troops to file past them without a sound until the two buildings were ringed. The officers, wearing bullet-proof garments, secreted themselves in the shadows, behind walls, in gardens.

Whispering into his shirt, John announced, "We're all sorted here. Still no sign of our man. We're going into Adamson's pad." He glanced at Brett and nodded towards the lifeless house.

On cue, the sky began to lighten. It was dawn. The operation was definitely underway.

Walking past the sad, immobile jalopy and nearing the front door, Big John extracted his gun. Brett was about to follow suit when he felt John's hand on his right arm. John breathed, "No. One's enough." Seeing Brett grimace, he added, "Keep it out of sight for now. If we're about to walk into an armed conflict, we may need an ace up our sleeves."

Brett queried, "Shouldn't guns be shown openly at all times?"

Not wanting an argument on the doorstep, John

197

was curt. "Don't quote the rule book at me! It's my neck on the block. I've told you my reasons."

Brett accepted John's judgement and made sure that the smart gun was hidden but accessible under his jacket.

John had considered all of the options. He could have brought in a strong-arm team to batter unceremoniously through the front door. He could have used a surreptitious and specialist lock-picker. He'd decided on the least dramatic approach. He stepped up to the door and yanked on the old-fashioned bell-pull. They waited for a minute that seemed like five and then tried again. "Heavy sleepers," he remarked. Inside the house, a clang reverberated hollowly.

Brett felt empty. The ominous lack of response alarmed him. At least Zoe and her uncle should have been in the building. And where was the guard that John had sent? Brett dreaded what they'd find inside.

Big John gave up. He tried the colossal knob but the door was locked. He peered into the keyhole and observed, "Key's in the lock." Looking to either side of the door, he selected a vulnerable window. Whispering into his shirt again, he said, "No answer. Going in through a window. Or rather, Brett is. He's more athletic than me."

With the butt of his gun, John smashed a diamond-shaped pane. He poked his hand through the hole and slipped the catch. Looking at Brett, he muttered, "There you are. In you go and open the front door."

With every second that passed, sunlight streamed more strongly into the valley. Birds started to chatter incessantly. Brett grabbed the sill and pulled himself up into the window frame. Swiftly, he let himself down into the lavish reception. The low sun also lit the sumptuous living room. "I'm in," Brett reported softly to his distant guardian angels. "Still no sign of life."

He made his way to the front door and unlocked it for his commanding officer. Without a sound, John stepped into the plush interior and surveyed the vulgar opulence. His right hand still held the smart gun. John waved in the direction of the kitchen and together they stepped cautiously towards it.

John swung open the door and peered inside. It was tidy. It did not look like a room in which a breakfast had just been prepared. The plates on the oak dresser were bone china, the glassware was lead crystal that caught the early sunshine and sparkled, and much of the kitchenware was polished silver.

Next, they tried the indulgent living room where almost every object was an antique. Clearly, the elder had spent a considerable amount of the village's bequest on luxuries for himself. The clunk of a huge grandfather clock repeated monotonously. On the mahogany furniture there were ornate vases, silver candlesticks and figurines where, in a normal house, there would have been a television and video recorder. The only obviously modern piece of equipment was a radio on one of the sideboards. It was deadly silent. Like the kitchen, the large lounge was deserted.

They tried each door in turn. The cloakroom, toilet and conservatory were all vacant. Everywhere Brett and Big John went, lush rugs of uninspiring colours muted the sound of their footfalls. "We're going upstairs," Brett informed the third wave. "No one downstairs."

The stairwell was extravagant on space and burnished wood. They could easily ascend the broad flight of stairs side by side. In the stillness, Brett could hear John wheezing before they were halfway up. At the top, there was a landing and balcony. The wall was decorated with oil paintings – probably portraits of generations of Adamsons. The four doors to the bedrooms were ajar. The fifth door led to an empty antiquated bathroom. No modern gadgets, no shower, no plastic.

Starting at one end of the landing, they pushed each door wide open and barged into the bedrooms. The first two contained beds like museum pieces – twice as large as necessary and covered with excessively elaborate eiderdowns. The quilts were unruffled, suggesting that no one had slept in the beds overnight. The dingy wardrobes and dressing tables were made of solid oak from a bygone age. "This stuff's been handed down for generations," John mumbled. "The place is worth a fortune."

Brett wasn't concerned with the value of the property. He was haunted by anxiety for Zoe. An unpleasant tingling invaded his body. His senses were heightened and his pulse drummed heavily.

The third bedroom was smaller, quaint, but similarly abandoned. Its walls were covered in sketches of the village and upland scenery. Brett recognized the tortoise rock in one of the drawings. Zoe's room. His nerves blazed. Her absence made his heart pound even more.

John hesitated outside the last bedroom and looked despondently at Brett. He had already come to the conclusion that they were on a wild-goose chase. He opened the final door and examined the room. Another enormous bedroom, small window, an amazing four-poster bed, but no incumbent.

John pointed to the bed and said, "I thought these things were only in old romances and horror films." Having drawn a complete blank, John relaxed. At the same time, he felt disappointed and irked. "No one's home," he reported at normal volume into his microphone. In the unoccupied house, his utterance sounded like a shout. "No Julie Penny, no constable, and no Adamsons. I doubt if the Adamsons are the type to treat themselves to a day trip to Skegness so I imagine they're holed up somewhere in the village. We're coming out."

They retraced their steps, down the ludicrous sweeping staircase, and out of the front door. The brilliance of the new day had dispelled the gloom over Upper Needless. It would take more than sunrise to dispel the gloom that had descended on

Brett. He feared that something was horribly wrong. Zoe's empty room reminded him of her vulnerability.

As they began to walk back towards the van, John muttered, "Any more bright ideas?"

Brett was not listening. "Look," he whispered, pointing to the ground in front of the village hall.

A police radio was lying like a discarded weapon at the base of the steps to the door.

Brett and John stared at the hall and then at each other. John spoke softly into his microphone, "There's a chance we've been looking in the wrong place. We're going to try the hall."

They walked stiffly the short distance to the wooden door, looking like cowboys in a hackneyed Western. There were three steps up to the doorway. Big John, still gripping his gun, paused and murmured, "We're going in now." To Brett, he breathed, "It's a flimsy door. If it doesn't open when I turn the handle, you clatter it. OK? I'll cover you if you go sprawling."

Brett nodded, flexed his shoulder and braced himself.

It was unnecessary. Big John pushed open the door at the first try and spilled into the hall, closely followed by Brett. At once both of them froze as they were greeted by an artificially cheerful voice. "I've been expecting you."

17

Brett gasped. He could never have prepared himself adequately for what he saw. On the platform, Thomas Adamson was standing over Zoe, holding a gun to her head and grinning. She was on her knees, gagged, petrified. Her blouse was torn and her hands were tied behind her back. Her face was bruised and swollen. Her arms bore cuts.

Brett shouted, "Don't you dare do anything else to her!"

Big John glanced at his apprentice and understood straightaway. To Brett, Zoe was much more than a precious witness. He had become entangled with her. Under his breath, John cursed. It was an extra burden that he could have done without.

Thomas laughed. "I don't think you're in much of a position to make demands." He was revelling in being several steps ahead of them.

Making sure that his team outside were kept in touch, John said, "Thomas Adamson, I presume. And Zoe."

Thomas peered at John and snapped, "Yes. Who are you?"

"Detective Superintendent Macfarlane."

"Ah! The big guns," he mocked. "And talking of big guns, I see you're armed."

"Yes," John replied. "What did you expect? In operations like this, the senior officer's always armed."

"And Detective Inspector Lawless?"

"You've got to be joking," John answered with apparent disdain. "He's too inexperienced. We don't put weapons in the hands of twenty-six year olds."

Thomas seemed to believe him. "OK, Superintendent Macfarlane," he snarled caustically. "Walk towards that window. The one that's open. Slowly," he demanded. Deliberately and threateningly, he brought his gun closer to Zoe's head. "That's right. No tricks or heroics, please." When John reached the window, he hissed, "Now, drop the gun out of the window."

Big John obeyed. He had no choice while Zoe was in Adamson's power. In the hush of dawn, they heard a thud as the weapon landed on the grass outside.

"Now close it," Thomas ordered.

Reluctantly, John pulled the window shut, isolating himself from his gun.

"That's better," Thomas cackled. "Now we can

get on with business," he said with derision.

From his new position by the window, John could see a policeman's body slumped against the wall. The young copper had been shot through the head. Under his breath, John swore miserably.

On the stage, Thomas Adamson snarled, "You must take me for a complete fool not to see the signs of betrayal in my own niece." He waved his gun towards her.

Brett tried to concentrate on Thomas, waiting for a moment of weakness, but his gaze kept flicking involuntarily to Zoe. He was scared for her. In fact he was terrified for her. He could feel the sweat on his forehead and palms and it trickled uncomfortably down his back, soaking into his shirt. Involuntarily, his thoughts turned to Derek Jacob's words. *"You'd often come up with a brilliant, complicated idea to explain something, and completely overlook the obvious simple answer."* He groaned inwardly. It *was* obvious. Thomas Adamson's house said it all. He lived in luxury. He was squandering the village's money on himself. He'd killed the wayward kids to preserve that cushy life. Zoe had said it all. *"He's nice as anything but he can change suddenly. He raves about God's will when the village is under threat."* Greedy and sick. Not Julie Penny. Thomas Adamson.

Big John had begun to ask questions. He wanted to hear answers – he wanted the third wave to record the answers – but he was also relying on the principle that killers rarely talk and shoot at the same time. It was a technique that Brett had come across in training. Keep him talking and his mind's not on firing.

"Why, Thomas? Why kill them?"

"It had to be done – to safeguard our way of life. Young people are the soul of the village. They're its future. I couldn't let that soul be torn out. Desertion has to be punished before it gathers momentum. They had to be made an example of."

Brett stared at Adamson. The elder was making excuses. He'd killed them because if the urge to leave Upper Needless had infected more of the village's young people, he would have forfeited the legacy that funded his excesses. Brett guessed that the inhabitants had always known the fate of the four youngsters but had suppressed it, refused to admit it or talk about it. Maybe they were so terrified of the elder that they did not dare to say anything. They simply went about their lives unquestioningly and numbly. Adamson's strategy had achieved exactly what he wanted. Total success and total loyalty. The village's silence ensured that Julie Penny heard nothing about the mini-rebellion and that the elder continued to receive the bequest. Zoe must have denied to herself that her uncle was capable of carrying out the ultimate punishment. For years, he'd acted as her father. She was so indebted to him that she'd banished from her mind any thought that he might have killed her friends. Now, as she knelt down helplessly like a trapped animal, grim reality was inescapable. It was reflected in her stunned eyes.

"Where did you kill them?" John queried. "Not in the wood."

"Here, in the hall. In the night or the early hours. Here, where I'm surrounded by friends."

While Adamson held his gun near Zoe and shifted his gaze rapidly from John to Brett and back again, Brett could not risk drawing his own gun.

"Why didn't you bury them in the village where you could make a proper job of it?"

"They were disgraced. Not worthy of the honour of a grave in my village. I put them in the car and dumped them away from here."

Big John nodded.

"And now," Adamson continued, "I've got to deal with the three of you." As he spoke, he became more animated, more self-righteous. "I've saved the village – no one here rebels any more – and I won't let you undo my work. It was justified. All it needed was a few martyrs. You should have been here to see it. All of it. Emma. You know, she was going with an outsider." He glanced with wild eyes at Brett. "Just like Zoe and you," he spat. "You should have heard Emma. She was screaming, 'Shoot me but not the baby. Please! He's done nothing wrong. It's not his fault. It's mine.' *Nothing wrong!*" Thomas screamed indignantly. "I waited till he was born, just in case he was one of ours, but he'd got the blood of strangers in him. I could tell. I could smell it. He was polluted." Suddenly, Adamson fixed his demented eyes on Brett and he barked, "Now *you've* polluted my village. You've polluted my niece. But I'm glad you've come back for her – your sweetheart," he snorted. "You can see what you've got her into. You can see the havoc you've caused." He hesitated cruelly. He was lingering over an enjoyable experience. "Upper Needless has told me what I must do. And you're privileged to witness the result of your interference. You can see for yourself how I punish those who seek to destroy us by mixing with strangers." He brought his gun to the side of Zoe's head.

Brett heard a muffled squeal from Zoe. She stared at him in fright, imploring him to save her.

"No!" Brett cried. "You said she was as good as a daughter to you. No one kills his own daughter."

"They would if the threat was sufficient, if there was enough at stake. You'd be surprised what humans can do when they're pushed to the limit. And that's what has happened here. Courtesy of your good self. You've brought it on. No one individual – not even Zoe – is more important than the village. There's got to be sacrifice for the common good."

For a second, Adamson took his eyes off Brett. Applying all of his attention to the execution, Thomas adjusted his position to make sure that the path of the bullet was true. He did not want any mistakes. He did not want the punishment to be messy and amateurish. He was putting on a show for Brett and John so it had to be done properly. With aplomb.

Released for an instant from Adamson's scrutiny, Brett knew that he would have to be fast and accurate. He would have to kill cleanly with a single shot. He tried to ignore Zoe's silent scream and focus solely on his duty. Yet he could not divorce himself from the fact that it was Zoe who was about to be sacrificed. He was nervous and trembling. He wasn't shooting at cardboard cutouts now. Perspiring freely, he delved inside his jacket and in one movement brought out the smart gun and aimed it. Thomas had twisted his body so that Brett did not have a clear sight of his chest. Instead he levelled the gun at Thomas's head and squeezed the trigger.

The shot resounded throughout the hall but, to Brett's sheer horror, his gun had not discharged. Only Thomas had fired. Grotesquely, Zoe was tossed sideways and slumped on to the platform. Blood poured liberally from her head.

Brett was utterly crushed. All he could see was Zoe's body. Discarded. All he could feel was numbness. He was incapacitated. It was only a moment, but that awful emptiness could have lasted for hours. And the damage that had been done would last a lifetime. If Brett *had* destroyed something precious as a child, he had just repeated the performance.

"Again!" John shouted.

Initially, Brett was too shocked to hear or comprehend. He stood in despair with his mouth open, unable to absorb the predicament or John's order.

"Again!" John screamed at him once more.

It was like being weighted down while struggling to reach the surface of a swimming pool. He needed air but the drag was unbearable and his body was drained of its strength and resolve. Then, out of the corner of his eye, he saw Thomas grinning insanely at him. He didn't hear the elder's words but he could see the amusement in his evil face and his lips mouthing, "What a pity. Your gun's jammed." Brett was racked with mental pain but suddenly he found the will to act. It was purely the capacity for revenge. He broke free of the weights, reached the surface and sucked in air. He took aim again.

The weapon felt slippery in his clammy hand. The quivering and moisture on his palms altered his normal grip. The pressure pattern of his hand was disguised and his fingerprint became unreadable. The chip did not recognize him. The smart gun was not smart enough. It denied that Brett was its owner. Again, it refused to fire. In the clinical and harmless atmosphere of practice, the smart gun was perfect. In the heat of a real operation when the life of another depended on it, the weapon was useless. Broken, Brett jettisoned the smart gun.

Thomas Adamson laughed like a madman. "Oh dear, oh dear," he bellowed sarcastically. "They've given you a gun that doesn't work. And just look at you! Devastated. Now you've seen what you're responsible for, you don't like it, do you?"

Brett had ceased to function. He gazed past

Adamson at Zoe. Thomas Adamson's gibe was the truth. Her death was Brett's fault.

"I've never punished outsiders before," Thomas said, walking slowly towards Brett, "but I've got no choice now. I've no need for a couple of hostages and an aeroplane to a safe haven. I've never wanted anything but Upper Needless. The village *is* my haven. But, left alive, you two would spoil it so I have to spoil you first." He halted three paces away from Brett.

Brett did not flinch. He did not even know if he cared now that Zoe was dead.

Thomas raised his weapon.

There was a crash as Big John's gun smashed through the window, accompanied by flying splinters of glass. The Superintendent lunged at his smart gun but he was too sluggish. It skidded across the floor and came to a halt near Thomas Adamson's feet. "Ah, a gift from heaven," he proclaimed. "A sign. It'll be a pleasure to kill you, Lawless, with a God-given gift." Eagerly, he bent down and picked it up.

Brett felt the cold barrel against his head, just above his left ear. He closed his eyes, shutting out the appalling image of Zoe, and waited.

Adamson delighted in pulling the trigger. He emitted a childlike giggle as he squeezed. But there was no other noise. Nothing happened. His temperament shifted abruptly and uncannily from ecstasy to annoyance and he yelled, "What's going on here?" He threw down John's smart gun and prepared to use his own weapon instead. The deranged smile returned to his face as he made ready to despatch Brett.

Before Adamson could fire, Big John had retrieved his weapon and trained it on Adamson. "No!" John growled. "You won't kill him. As soon as I see your trigger finger begin to twitch – or even if I think it's about to twitch – you're dead. The merest movement and I fire. So just back off and drop the gun."

Thomas groaned theatrically and twisted his face towards John. "Please, don't patronize me. I'm not a simpleton. Your gun doesn't work and you know it," he mocked.

"No," Big John replied coolly. "Sometimes they give me police officers who don't work but the guns do – only too well." As always, his head was clear. His hand was steady and free of perspiration.

"Full marks for bluffing," Adamson retorted. "But first I kill your lovesick colleague here and then I kill you. It will be a pleasure."

"I warn you again," John hissed. "Don't do it."

"You're a fool, Detective Superintendent Macfarlane." Disregarding him, Thomas turned back towards Brett. His next victim.

Big John was calm and collected. He had tunnel vision. His eyes narrowed on Thomas Adamson's head and right forefinger. Everything else dissolved.

A second later, as soon as Adamson began to squeeze the trigger, John fired twice.

The first bullet entered Adamson's right ear and

the second parted the hair that grew in front of his ear. One of the bullets burst from his shattered left cheek with bits of bone and blood. The other lodged in his brain. Just before he died, he bleated with surprise. It was the last sound that the killer made. He dropped to the floor like a puppet whose strings had been cut.

John did not have to examine Adamson's body. He knew that he had done what was required of him. He bowed his head to speak into the miniature microphone. "We're OK," he said. "I repeat. We're both OK. It's over. Thomas Adamson's down and –" He glanced at Brett's distraught face before adding, "So is Zoe Adamson. Get the third wave and forensic team in here but give us five minutes to sort ourselves out."

John guided Brett to one of the hard wooden seats. "I'm sorry, Brett," he said gently. "Sorry about Zoe. What can I say? I've bought you five minutes to compose yourself before the vultures come in. That's all. I can't do any more."

Brett looked at the Superintendent absently and murmured, "I need to touch her."

John shook his head. "You know the rules. You can't."

"I need to see her. I need to say goodbye. I want to hold her hand."

"It's still not allowed, Brett. Nothing is disturbed till forensics have done their stuff. Now I'm going to busy myself with Thomas Adamson, the policeman over there and the weapons. I don't have time to keep an eye on you. As far as I'm concerned, you just sit here recovering."

Brett looked at John, but the Superintendent turned his back intentionally. It took a while for John's insinuation to sink in. "Thanks," Brett mumbled.

It required all of Brett's courage to walk between the rows of seats and mount the stage. But he had to do it. He could not possibly trudge away from Upper Needless without taking his leave of her.

He knelt down beside her. The wounds and the gag had taken away her beauty, but they couldn't take away Brett's memory of her vitality. He couldn't hold her hands because they were tied behind her. He ached to untie them, to give her the semblance of freedom and humanity, but he knew that he couldn't. Without disturbing her body, he touched her upper left arm where the torn material had exposed it. Her flesh was still warm and supple. Her circulation and all metabolic activity had ceased, he knew, but for a short while she could still feel alive. Brett swallowed and whispered, "I'm sorry, Zoe. Really sorry." For a split second, he thought that he recalled apologizing to someone else, many years ago. In a flash, he was a child again, bewildered and fearful. He sensed another death. Then the elusive recollection evaporated and he was left only with Zoe. Before he let go of her, he muttered, "Bye, love."

Hurt, angry, remorseful and puzzled, he stood up and took a deep breath.

The doors to the hall opened like floodgates. Suddenly, the place was swarming with police officers and scientists.

Brett heard John thunder, "Who gave the order to throw the gun in through the window?"

Clare, on her way towards Brett, stopped in her tracks. "I didn't like the way it was going," she said. "I gave the order. I'll take the rap."

"That's not all you'll take," Big John replied. "You'll take my undying gratitude. Well done."

Clare beamed at him but then turned again towards Brett. All trace of her smile had disappeared. She went to him, glanced at Zoe's pitiful body and then squeezed his arm. "I'm sorry," she stammered. "There wasn't anything else you could do."

Trying to preserve his dignity, Brett nodded solemnly. But he knew that it wasn't true. None of this would have happened if he had not fallen for her. And now she had fallen for him.

Big John joined them and suggested to Brett, "Why don't you take a walk? Get some fresh air. We've got enough hands to finish off here."

Brett did not wish to shirk his obligations but neither did he wish to disgrace himself in front of the team. "OK," he mumbled. "Thanks."

Starchily, he walked through the commotion of note-taking, measurements, dusting, the covering of the windows ready for the search for old blood stains by laser. He opened the door, breathed the country air and with relief stepped unsteadily outside.

Inside, John called to the electronics technician, "Brett's still wired. Go to the van and turn it off. That's an order. I don't think we need to record him just now."

Without hesitation, Brett strode down the lane, through the waking, bemused village and past the parked vehicles. As he went, an officer called to him, saying, "We've just detained Mrs Julie Penny. Says she's on her way to visit Thomas Adamson in Upper Needless."

"Let her go," Brett replied absently. "She's got nothing to do with it."

Leaving behind the puzzled officers, Brett began to climb mechanically towards the uplands. He clambered up Zoe's hill at a reckless pace till the blood throbbed painfully in his head. He was drained but he did not stop to rest until he reached the stones at the summit of Horsehill Tor. He surveyed the view, the angry old man, the startled tortoise, the wrinkly woman and then he collapsed. In the vast lonely Peaks there was no one to watch his disintegration. His tears fell on to Zoe's sacred ground.

Keith tapped the bundle of papers and said, "Thanks, John. A very full and frank report as always. And, once again, an investigation brought to a satisfactory conclusion. Very satisfactory. It won't harm your case for promotion at all."

"Mmm," John replied sceptically. "I wish *I* was satisfied. It was untidy. And it'd be wrong to give me much credit. One: three people died in the final operation. That shouldn't have happened. Two: I didn't crack the case. You may not like to admit it after his little indiscretion, but Brett Lawless is the one who led us to Adamson."

"So I read," Keith admitted. "I told you at the outset that he was good. But I also read some things about him that worry me. He seems somewhat accident prone. The business with Glenn Troke. Going to pieces with the gun at the end. Disobeying your orders." He paused before asking, "Any idea why he had the problem with the smart gun? I don't mean technically. Since the problem, Diana's discovered that excessive sweating confuses the recognition chip. It's back to the drawing board with that. But why did he get so nervous? He doesn't strike me as the hot-headed sort."

John coughed and muttered, "No idea."

The Chief Superintendent's face creased. "Did you put *everything* in the report, John?"

John did his best to look surprised. "You know me," he retorted. "Thorough."

"Yes," Keith replied, still not convinced but unwilling to interrogate John any further.

"Perhaps he's just touchy with guns," John suggested. "That's not a bad thing in my book." He could not bring himself to jeopardize Brett's career by reporting that, foolishly, Brett had allowed himself to fall in love with a witness. He was suffering enough for his mistake without it ending up in an official report. When he'd written it John had decided to overlook the possibility that, if Brett had not got so involved with Zoe, he might have kept his cool and not befuddled the smart gun's chip. John's account ascribed the unfortunate loss of life purely to equipment failure.

"OK," Keith said, knowing that John would reveal nothing else. "What's your recommendation?"

John shrugged. "Well, if I were in your place..."

"Which you're not – yet."

"No," John responded, trying to disguise the regret in his tone. "Anyway, I'd say he's ready for his own cases. They'd have to be the right ones, though. Ones where he can exploit his strengths."

"And what are the right ones?"

"He's a scientist at heart. He'd work well on any case with lots of forensic input."

"The cranky cases?"

"Someone's got to solve them. Brett's a good logical thinker. He'll come up with plenty of ideas."

"What about his weaknesses? Before, you said he'd need the right partner to supply what he lacks. You reckoned he'd need someone who works well with people."

"That's right," John estimated. "He's no judge of character – not yet, anyway. He needs someone with a good nose for villains. Someone who'll supply the down-to-earth common sense to hold him in check – or he'll be all clever theories and no arrests."

"I gather you have someone in mind."

Big John grinned and nodded. "Of course. Clare Tilley's a promising and willing police officer. Not academic, but solid. Feet on the ground, but with initiative. In time, she's serious promotional material. She did a good job on the Adamson case. I've got her to thank for being here. So's Brett. And she gets on well with him."

Keith frowned. "Not a romance, is it? That's the last thing we need between partners."

"No," John stated definitely. He knew that after

Zoe, Brett would have learnt his lesson. He doubted that Brett would recover for some time. Zoe would always be there – just under his skin. "They just seem to have hit it off, as friends and colleagues. Nothing more. All perfectly healthy."

"All right," Keith said, bringing their session to an end. "I'll think about it. Lawless and Tilley, eh? We'll see. I'll talk to Brett Lawless this afternoon."

"You've taken a bit of leave to clear your head after this Adamson case," the Chief Superintendent commented.

"Yes, thanks. It was helpful," Brett said, standing stiffly by the large desk. He still felt bruised and battered but he did not say so. He did not reveal that, in his two weeks of leave, he had considered quitting the police force. That was his immediate reaction to Zoe's execution. He recoiled from life and work. But he was not a quitter. He soon realized that giving up would not bring her back. He decided to carry on. If he had resigned he would have wasted his life on regrets and despondency. The usual prescription for bereavement was hard work. It was supposed to offer him distraction. It was supposed to help him forget. But he didn't want to forget her. He resolved to work away the guilt that entangled him, but to preserve his memory of Zoe.

Keith weighed a document in his left hand. "John's account of the case and your first school report," he explained.

Brett said nothing. He waited for the criticism, wondering how severe it was going to be.

Keith put down the dossier and said, "Not bad. Even good in places. John's made it very clear in here that it was your inquiries that led to Adamson. Even so, could do better." The Chief rested his elbows on his desk and brought his forefinger and thumb together so that they were almost touching. "In disobeying John's orders, you came this close," he declared aggressively, "to mutiny and high treason; this close to a severe reprimand, but..." He spread his hands again, ending the admonition for the moment. "Well, there are some big pluses in here as well as big minuses. And there's something else that John's not telling me. But if John's covering up for you, I can only assume he doesn't want to hold you back. That means you *must* be good. Not everyone gets John's seal of approval. So, I won't hold an inquiry, but we must find some time soon for a full debriefing. For now, there's a sentence to pass on you. It's good news. I'm going to assign you to your own cases. You'll be in charge. But you won't be entirely on your own. You'll have an assistant. After careful thought, I've decided that Clare Tilley's going to partner you. Does that cause you any problems?"

"No, sir. Not at all. I'm very pleased."

"Good. That's all for the moment, Detective Inspector Lawless. I guess you're going to stay with us. Welcome aboard."

Brett raised a smile. "Thank you, sir," he said.

Look out for the second

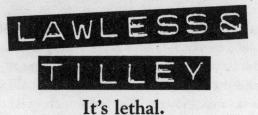

It's lethal.

Deep Waters

THE CASE : Colin Games has died after a bizarre illness. A post-mortem reveals no obvious cause of death, but the pathologist isn't happy. Enlarged liver, anaemia, heart irregularities – it all points to *poison*...

For Lawless and Tilley, the answer lies in the pharmaceutical industry. For who knows more about poisons than chemists? And some of Games's best friends were chemists...

The third Lawless & Tilley is coming soon:
MAGIC EYE
It's an enigma.